JESSICA BECK

CAST IRON SUSPICION

THE FIFTH CAST IRON COOKING MYSTERY

D1528484

This one, as usual, is for P and E, my reasons why.

When Annie's ex-boyfriend, Timothy Roberts, is found dead in his burned-out cabin, she is considered a suspect by the whole town, particularly since Timothy dumped her not that long ago. The victim's current girlfriend, Jenna Lance, is missing, so the twins, Pat and Annie Marsh, start digging into the man's life, and his death, in an effort to figure out who might have done it. Is Jenna a killer on the run? Is Timothy's no-good brother to blame? Or did one of his clients decide to write him off permanently as a bad debt? As the twins struggle to figure out who closed the books on the accountant and balanced his books forever, they end up uncovering more secrets than they ever expected to find.

CHAPTER 1: PAT

OUR HOMECOMING WASN'T NEARLY AS joyous as my twin sister, Annie, and I had hoped for after being away from Maple Crest for a few days visiting our Aunt Della. As we pulled into the Cast Iron Store and Grill parking lot after a long and tiring drive, we were surprised to find Jenna Lance and Timothy Roberts sitting together on the front porch waiting for us. My initial reaction was one of pleasant surprise, but then I noticed the dire expressions on both their faces. Why did they both look so grim? I'd started dating Jenna at the same time Annie had begun to see Timothy, and I had high expectations for both relationships.

Unfortunately, those expectations were about to die.

"Pat, we need to talk," Jenna told me solemnly as I got out of Annie's car to greet her. I'd heard that tone of voice from a woman before, though not from her, and I knew without much doubt what it meant. Whatever we'd once had was clearly about to come to a sudden and abrupt end.

"Annie, that's why I'm here, too," Timothy added. They both looked as though someone dear to them had just died.

"Do you mind taking a walk with me?" Jenna asked me. She clearly wanted some privacy to dump me, but I was in no mood to make it any easier for her.

"The truth of the matter is that I'm kind of beat. I don't feel much like taking a walk at the moment," I said. It was an accurate statement, but the real reason I didn't want to have a chat that very second was that I wasn't all that excited about the prospect of being discarded like yesterday's newspaper. "Can I take a rain check? How about if we talk tomorrow instead?"

"No, I'm sorry, but this can't wait. It needs to be right now," she said firmly.

Apparently I wasn't going to get even the slightest reprieve. I was in no particular mood to be let down easy, though. "Jenna, if you're going to dump me, just go ahead and do it. It's not as though Annie hasn't seen it happen to me before." Granted, the last time it had happened had been in seventh grade, so this would be a new experience for me to go through it as an adult.

"Is that why you're here with her?" Annie asked Timothy in disbelief. "Are you breaking up with me, too?"

Annie had clearly been caught off guard by this development as well. Why had the two of them chosen to end their relationships with us immediately upon our return to Maple Crest, and together, at that? There was only one reason I could think of, and I didn't much care for it. "Hang on a second," I said. "You two aren't ditching us so that *you* can be together, are you?" I asked them.

Timothy's face turned instantly red, and Jenna wouldn't even look in my direction.

Apparently I'd scored a direct hit.

"Seriously? You've got to be kidding me! How long ago did this happen? Pat and I haven't been gone that long," Annie said angrily.

"When you know something isn't right, and when something is, time isn't that much of a factor," Timothy said softly, clearly trying to calm her down. That was a big mistake, but I wasn't in the mood to help him out with my sister.

"And you're saying that we weren't right?" Annie asked fiercely. "That wasn't your attitude just before we left town, or do I need to remind you?"

"That won't be necessary; there's nothing wrong with my memory," Timothy said sternly. That was the wrong thing to do as well, but again, I didn't say a word. I had my own problems.

"I still can't believe this is happening," I said, having a hard time grasping the concept that our significant others had fallen for each other, and so quickly.

"When you two left to help your aunt, Timothy and I decided to have dinner together, just to keep each other company while you were gone," Jenna explained in near tears. I couldn't blame her. I wasn't too pleased about the situation, either. "Something clicked between us instantly, and we knew that we belonged together from that moment on. Neither one of us meant to hurt you."

"Well, it's a little too late to start worrying about that now, isn't it?" Annie asked. "You know what? I don't see any reason at all to continue this conversation. I'm going home. Pat, I'll see you in the morning," my sister added as she stomped off toward her vehicle.

"Hang on, Annie. Can't we at least discuss this like adults?" Timothy asked her. "You know as well as I do that we haven't been dating all that long, and besides, sometimes these things just happen."

My twin sister gave him a sour look before she spoke. "I get it, Timothy," she said. "We're through. Why in the world would I want to talk about it any more than we already have?"

"I just don't want things to be awkward between us going forward," he said.

Annie shot him a grin that had no joy in it whatsoever. "Good luck with that, and be sure to let me know how it goes on your end."

"So, does that mean that we *can't* be friends?" he asked.

"What do you think?" she replied. "I don't know how Pat feels, but I've already got plenty of friends. I don't need any more at the moment, but I'll keep you in mind if a slot opens up. How does that sound? *Friends*," she repeated with a snort of derision.

"Do you feel that way, too, Pat?" Jenna asked me.

"I do. I agree with my sister," I said as I grabbed my bag and pulled out my keys to the Iron. "Thanks for stopping by and letting us know, but there's no reason to continue this conversation. Your minds are obviously made up. Good luck to you both." The last bit was thrown in without any real sincerity behind it, and what was more, everyone present knew it.

"Pat, don't be that way," Jenna pled.

"Sorry, but at the moment, it's the best I can do."

"Come on, Jenna. Let's go," Timothy said as he gently took her hand in his. I felt a stab of jealousy at how comfortably he did it, and how readily she accepted the gesture. "I told you this was a bad idea," he added softly. So that explained why only Timothy's truck had been in the parking lot when we'd arrived. Naturally the two of them had come together to cut us loose.

Annie shook her head when she saw the gesture, whether in anger or disgust I couldn't tell, and she got into her Subaru and drove away. As she left, she kicked up a bit of gravel on the way out, but who could blame her for wanting to get out of there as quickly as she could?

"Well, at least you were right about it being a bad idea," I said as I retreated into the store and locked the door behind me. I couldn't stop them from coming back to the Iron the next day, but I *could* keep them out for now, and at the moment, that was *all* that I cared about.

I had taken four steps inside the Grill when my cell phone rang. I half expected it to be Jenna, a call that I wasn't about to answer, but it was Annie instead. "Hey, sis."

Without preamble, she asked me, "Pat, did you see that coming?"

"No, I was just as blindsided as you were," I admitted. "Are you okay?"

"I was about to ask you the exact same thing," she said. "Everyone knows that you're the more sensitive one of us."

"Who thinks that?" I asked, though after giving it a moment's thought, I knew that it was probably true. It wasn't that my sister didn't have a heart; it was just that I tended to wear mine on my sleeve, whereas she'd been known to bury her emotions instead of displaying them for the whole world to see.

"Everybody," she said. "The real question is what are we going to do about it?"

4

"Annie, there's nothing we *can* do," I said. "If they don't want to be with us, do we really *want* them in our lives?"

There was a long pause on the other end before she answered. "No. Of course not. For a second there I had the stupid notion that Timothy was worth fighting for, but you're right. Even if I got him back, things would never be the same between us again."

"Sis, maybe in the long run, this is best for everyone," I said.

"In what world could that possibly be true?" she asked me.

"Think about it. It could have been much worse. What if we'd married them, and *then* they'd discovered that they belonged together?"

"Pat, excuse me for saying so, but right now I don't want to look on the bright side of anything. I just want to wallow a bit, lick my wounds, and then deal with being rejected in my own way. How humiliating."

"For which one of us?"

"I'd have to say both, in equal portions," she answered. "At least we won't have to see them together in our store."

Was she serious? "Annie, be realistic. We're just about the only choice they have for buying a great many things without leaving town to do it, not to mention them needing to get their mail. They both have PO boxes here, or did you forget? You know as well as I do that sooner or later they're going to come in together, so we might as well deal with it now."

"I'm putting laxative in their coffees if they try to order anything at my grill," she said angrily, and then, after a moment, she laughed. "And I'll be sure to lock the bathroom doors first."

"Maybe you should just think about doing it instead of actually carrying through with that plan," I said, relieved that at least a bit of Annie's ire was dissipating. I was hurt and angry myself, but I could control my emotions better than my twin sister could, at least to the point of not spiking anyone else's drink with laxative, but I wasn't sure my sister could say that.

"I was just kidding," Annie said a little defensively. "I would never do that."

"Because they'd know instantly who did it, or because it would be the wrong thing to do?"

"Would it be horrible if I said that maybe it was a little bit of both?" she asked me.

"No, for tonight, that's fine. How's this going to affect you two being neighbors?" Timothy had built his new cabin on a large parcel of land next to Annie's with a windfall of money he'd gotten recently, thanks in good part to us.

"We're separated by some pretty thick woods, so I doubt that it's going to be an issue," she said. Taking a softer tone, she asked me, "Pat, is there something wrong with us?"

"No. Of course not. Why would you even ask me that?"

"Oh, I don't know. We just got dumped at the same time in front of one another. Does that sound normal to you?"

"Of course not, but you've got to remember that it wasn't because of anything we did," I said. "Don't worry, Annie. We're going to get through this."

"I know, but I still want to take a little time and pout about it before I'm ready to accept it."

"Agreed," I said, and then a groan slipped out.

"What was that for?"

"I just realized that by tomorrow morning, everyone in town is going to know that we got dumped side by side," I said.

"Including Molly, you mean," Annie said. Once upon a time, I'd believed that Molly Fennel was the love of my life, but she'd ended up breaking my heart. I still carried a torch for her though, no matter what my current life's circumstances might be.

"Yes, even Molly," I said.

"It will be okay, Pat," Annie said. "We're going to get through this."

"Hey, that was the exact same advice I just gave to you," I pointed out.

"Yeah, but I said it a lot better than you did," she said with the hint of a laugh in her voice. "See you in the morning."

"Call me if you need to talk later tonight," I told her.

"Thanks, but I'm going to annihilate a pint of chocolate ice cream, and then I'm going to bed. I suggest you do the same."

"I may substitute something else for the ice cream, but I like the way you think."

"Good night, baby brother."

"Good night, big sister," I said. Even if it was only by seven minutes, it was still true that she'd been born first, and Annie often reminded me of it. We were both close to Kathleen—our truly older sister, and the sheriff for our county—but there was a special bond between Annie and me that couldn't be denied.

"See you in the morning," I said.

"You can count on it," she replied.

It took us both a while to deal with what happened, but by the time a month had passed, the wounds had started to heal, and a month after that, Annie and I could see them together without cringing. It didn't hurt that the couple had been fighting more and more lately, and everyone in town could see that a breakup was imminent.

But before that could happen, someone up and killed Timothy Roberts at his cabin, and at that instant, everything changed for all of us.

CHAPTER 2: ANNIE

THE NIGHT TIMOTHY DIED, MY nightmares had been more vivid than I could ever recall them being in my life. One in particular haunted me as I fought to sleep. I dreamed I was sitting waist-deep in an old crone's cauldron, slowly being boiled alive, when I suddenly awoke to the very real sound of sirens wailing in the distance and the bitter taste of acrid smoke in the air. Something was on fire, and my best guess was that it was nearby! I immediately thought of the woods that surrounded my cabin and how dry the weather had been lately. Had some errant spark lit my land afire? After leaping out of bed, I took a moment to assess the situation before I jumped to any conclusions. True, there was smoke in the air, but it wasn't close.

At least not close enough.

Not yet, anyway. The sirens were in the distance as well.

Apparently I had a little time before I needed to start panicking.

I glanced at the clock and saw that it was a little past two in the morning. There was a new moon in the sky that offered little help for night vision, so I flipped on the lights and got dressed quickly, pulling on my boots last and forgoing my usual tennis shoes. In the short amount of time it took me to get dressed, the sirens had grown louder. As I rushed outside, I looked around for any sign that my land was ablaze.

No flames—or even dancing embers—were within sight of my cabin or my land.

But the smoke was clearly coming from nearby.

There was only one other cabin in my part of the woods, so it didn't take any great leap to realize that Timothy Roberts's land must be burning, perhaps even his brand-new cabin itself. Though he'd broken up with me a few months earlier and there was still a touch of bitterness in my heart toward him, it was time to put our differences aside and see if there was anything I could do to help.

Racing through the woods toward his place would have been insanity itself in the darkness that enveloped me. I knew the forest around me better than anyone else alive, but there was just too much underbrush and other obstacles to navigate on foot in the dark. I'd considered putting in a walking path between our cabins when we'd first started dating, but naturally enough, that idea had died along with our budding relationship.

Grabbing my keys and locking the cabin door behind me, I got into my Subaru and made my way down the twisting path that served as my driveway. Once I was out on the main road, it was a matter of driving half a mile north to get to Timothy's turnoff.

I didn't get very far up it, though. His driveway was blocked by one of my sister's deputies. I knew him on sight, as I did every other police officer in the Maple Crest force. "Hey, Hank. Could you let me past?"

"I'm sorry, Annie, but I've got orders to let only emergency vehicles through. You understand, don't you?"

I knew my sister had given him his orders directly, but I wasn't going to let that stop me. It was time to go straight to the top.

I pulled out my cell phone and dialed her number. "Hey, Kathleen. I'm here, and Hank won't let me by."

"I was just about to call you. Annie, there's nothing you can do here, so you might as well turn around and go back home." She sounded tired and more than a little upset.

"Have they managed to contain the fire yet?" I asked, ignoring her advice.

"Nearly," she said. "Fortunately it didn't spread very far. Don't worry; your cabin and your land should both be safe."

That was good to know, but it wasn't my main concern at the

moment. "How's Timothy? He must be really upset. I'd at least like to say hello and offer whatever I can to help him."

"I'm afraid you can't do that," she said, and I could hear a sudden deadness in her voice.

"Is he okay?" I asked hesitantly. While the man hadn't turned out to be the love of my life, I still didn't wish ill of him. At least not on this epic scale.

"Annie, I'm afraid he didn't make it," Kathleen said somberly.

I couldn't believe what she was telling me. "What? He's *dead*? What happened? Kathleen, please tell Hank to let me through right now, because if you don't, I'm going straight home, grabbing a flashlight, and crashing through the woods to get there, and there's nothing you can do to stop me."

She knew better than to argue with me. "Give me one second."

"That's about *all* of the time you've got before I force my way there," I said, trying to come to grips with this new reality.

"Pat should really be with you right now," Kathleen said.

"Well, he's not, and I'm not about to wait around until he shows up. Make the call, sis."

The line died abruptly as Hank's walkie-talkie jumped to life. "Let my sister through, Hank," I heard her instruct him.

"Yes, ma'am. You told me yourself not to let anyone past. That's why I kept her from coming up," he apologized.

"And now I'm telling you to allow her in," she answered curtly. She was clearly in no mood to be trifled with.

Neither was I.

The radio died, and Hank looked sheepishly at me. "You can go on up. It wasn't personal, Annie."

"I know that," I said, and then I jumped back into my car and drove up Timothy's driveway. He had chosen a much more sensible path from the road to his place than I had mine, and his short drive led me around one corner and into the clearing where he'd built his cabin.

My stomach dropped as I took it all in. The place was a charred mess. Half the roof was gone, and a handful of volunteer firefighters were periodically dousing what remained of it with water from their pumper trucks. Every now and then, a spark would leap upward, and they'd extinguish it before it could do any further damage. The woods immediately around the house were black and burned and also quite soggy from their efforts.

My house, and even my land, may have been safe, but everything Timothy owned, including his life, was now gone.

———⊷⧫⧫⊷———

I parked my Subaru out of the way and got out of my car. As I started toward the burned-out shell of the cabin, Kathleen came striding purposefully toward me. "You can't go in there, Annie. There's nothing anyone could have done to save him. By the time the alarm sounded, he was most likely already gone."

"Why didn't I smell smoke sooner?" I asked, unable to keep my gaze from the charred remains of what had once been a beautiful cabin. It was never going to be livable again; that much was clear.

"The wind was coming from the opposite direction, something you should thank your lucky stars for. It kept the fire, as well as the smoke, from spreading toward you."

"Where is he?" I choked out. "Was he alone?"

She pointed to a pair of EMTs zipping up a body bag, and I started toward it before my sister grabbed my arm. "Don't do it, Annie."

"I want to see him," I said, resisting her grip.

She was too strong for me, though. "The truth of the matter is that there's not much left to see. And yes, he was alone, at least as far as we've been able to determine so far. It's barely safe in there now for the inspector, but the fire chief was able to at least determine that there was only one person inside."

"What's the fire inspector doing in there?" I asked, not putting it together quite yet.

"What I'm about to tell you is confidential," she said. "Look at me, Annie. I mean it."

"I can at least tell Pat, can't I?"

"Yes, but no one else."

"Right now, as far as I'm concerned, there *is* no one else."

Kathleen sighed heavily then hesitated another moment before she answered, "From the inspector's preliminary findings, there's not much doubt that the fire was deliberately set."

I couldn't believe what I was hearing. "Someone burned Timothy to death on purpose?" I asked in anguish. It sounded like a horrible way to die, and I certainly didn't wish that fate on my ex-boyfriend, or anyone else, for that matter.

"That we don't know," she said. "Whether he was still alive or already dead at the time of the arson is yet to be determined."

"Why would anyone do it?"

"One theory is that they were trying to cover up another crime. Annie, we need to explore the possibility that he very well might have already been dead before the first match was ever struck."

CHAPTER 3: PAT

I was awakened by a phone call in the middle of the night, something that rarely meant good news in my experience. "Pat, wake up. I need you."

It was my older sister, Kathleen, and I couldn't imagine the circumstances in which she would ever need me for anything, let alone in the dead of night. "What's going on, sis?"

"There was a fire at Timothy Roberts's place. I'm afraid he's dead, Pat."

"What happened?" I asked, trying to force myself awake. "Does Annie know?"

"Hank's got her sitting at the bottom of Timothy's driveway at the moment, but we both know that's not going to last very long. She's going to need your strength, Pat. How soon can you get here?"

"I'm on my way right now," I said.

I was starting to hang up when she said, "I'll call Hank and tell him to let you straight through. There's one more thing, Pat."

What could be added to the bad news I'd already heard? As I pulled on my jeans, I asked her, "What is it?"

"I can't say for sure yet, but it's looking more and more like Timothy was murdered."

"Why would anyone want to kill him? Besides Annie, I mean." I'd added the last bit without thinking, but I knew that it would be a conclusion that some of the folks around town would no doubt be leaping to when they heard the news. After all, my sister hadn't taken their breakup well, not that I'd been a sterling example of good manners myself with Jenna. The way they'd done it had been unfortunate, to say

Jessica Beck

the least, and it had taken Annie and me some time to put it past us. "Strike that. Does Jenna know what happened?"

"I'm not sure. We can't seem to find her," Kathleen said. "Now, do you want to keep talking to me, or do you want to get over here and take care of our sister?"

"Bye," I said as I hung up the phone and threw on a T-shirt. As I drove toward Timothy's place, I couldn't help but wonder how Annie was going to take the news. Before they'd dated, she and Timothy had been good friends, so he'd been in her life for quite a while. Driving through the darkness, I knew that all I could do was be there for my twin sister. I understood that there were no words of real comfort I could offer her, but my presence was probably the best thing I could give her at the moment. Annie needed me, and I was going to her. It was as simple as that, and if Kathleen neglected to tell Hank to let me pass by, then he was going to have a fight on his hands, and I didn't care if he was armed or not, even if he was old enough to be my father.

Fortunately, I didn't have to find out; Hank waved me through the second he saw me.

I pulled my truck in beside Annie's Subaru and got out to join her. Kathleen was saying something to her, and from Annie's expression, I knew that she was just getting the news that Timothy's death had been deliberate. The overpowering smells emanating from the extinguished fire were awful, and I tried not to think about what they were composed of as I approached Annie.

"Hey, sis. I'm so sorry," I said as I put an arm around her.

Annie mumbled something and pulled herself into me.

Kathleen took it all in, and then she nodded her thanks to me for coming before she spoke. "I'll tell you more when I find out what's going on, but right now I need to deal with this crime scene."

Annie nodded numbly, and Kathleen took that as permission to leave us. Our big sister might have been the sheriff in these parts, and a very important person, but it was clear she was happy about turning our sister over to me.

"Are you okay?" I asked Annie softly. "I'm having a hard time believing all of this."

"Someone killed him, Pat," she said as she buried her face in my chest.

I stroked her back. "I heard."

"Who would do something like that?"

"I have no idea," I answered.

"They can't find Jenna. Did you hear?"

I pulled away for a moment. "Yes, but surely she's not involved. Does Kathleen think *she* might have done it?" The idea was hard for me to even consider. Jenna was a kind person at heart, with a love for both people and animals that extended well beyond her veterinary practice and her daily life. I couldn't imagine the circumstances that would push her to murder another human being.

"I have no idea, but everyone in town knows how much they've been fighting lately," Annie said.

"Couples fight all of the time," I said. "But that doesn't necessarily mean that Jenna had anything to do with this." I swept an arm around the wreckage that had so recently been Timothy Roberts's life.

"I know, but it's suspicious, don't you think?"

"I don't even want to consider the possibility," I said.

Annie pulled away and looked up at me. "But we have to, don't we?"

"What do you mean?"

"Pat, everyone knows that Timothy and I had a bad breakup. Not only that, but my place is just through the woods over there," she said as she pointed toward her home.

"Annie, that was months ago. No one's going to think you did it. Too much time has passed."

"Do you honestly believe that?" she asked me intently.

I thought about it, and I knew that she was probably right. As much as I loved our fellow townsfolk, gossip seemed to be the main hobby around town, and while I knew that Jenna's name would be taken in vain quite a bit in the coming days, Annie's wouldn't be left out of the mix.

For that matter, I would probably be a suspect as well, given the fact that the man had stolen my girlfriend so publicly. I hated that expression. He couldn't have stolen her if she hadn't wanted him more than she'd wanted me. But would most folks look at it that way? I had a sinking feeling that Annie and I were both going to be involved in this up to our eyebrows soon enough, whether we liked it or not. "Kathleen's not going to be happy about it," I said lamely.

"I'm sure she'll find a way to live with her disappointment," Annie said. "The first thing we need to do is find Jenna."

"Don't you think Kathleen is going to want to handle that herself?" I asked. "After all, she has the resources to track people down. We don't."

"You're right," Annie said, but I didn't even get a chance to relish the minor victory before she added, "While she's hunting Jenna down, we need to dig into Timothy's life to see who else might want to wish him harm."

"If you would have asked me this morning if Timothy Roberts had *any* enemies, I would have been hard pressed to name names."

"Besides us, you mean," Annie said.

"You know what I mean. Who would want an accountant dead?"

She shook her head. "You're kidding, right? What if he was cooking the books for some bad guy? Wouldn't that give them a motive to get rid of him? Especially if he threatened to talk?"

"Do you honestly think Timothy would be an accountant for bullies and thugs?" I asked her.

"Bad people can still wear suits and talk as though they are civilized. Maybe he caught someone doing something they shouldn't have been doing, and he threatened to expose them."

"It's probably worth looking into, but how are we going to find out?"

"That part's easy," Annie said. "We need to go speak with Robin before Kathleen has a chance to." Robin Jenkins was Timothy's secretary/personal assistant, and no one alive knew Timothy's clientele better than she did.

"Right now?" I asked her, watching as the firemen doused another errant ember.

"What better time is there? Besides, she has the right to know what happened to her boss."

"Fine," I said, knowing that there was no use arguing with her when she'd made up her mind about something. "Let's go. Should we take your car or my truck?"

"Let's get them both out of here. We'll drop your truck off at the store, and then we can go together in my Subaru." Annie glanced back at the gutted shell one last time. "I can't believe he's gone."

"I can't, either. I'm sorry. I know that you cared a great deal for him once upon a time."

"I did, but that's not the only reason I want to find his killer. I can already hear the whispers behind our backs. We need to solve Timothy's murder, and we need to do it quickly, Pat."

"I'm not disagreeing. I only hope that Jenna is okay."

"I'm sure she's fine," Annie said, but I didn't believe her, and I suspected that she doubted the words herself.

We walked over to Kathleen. "We're leaving," I said.

She looked surprised by the news. "Really?"

Annie glanced at the burned-out structure. "You're right. There's nothing we can do here."

"Why do I have the feeling that you're giving up entirely too easily?" Kathleen asked her.

"What can I say? Sometimes you make sense," Annie said, and then—whether it was for our sister's sake or it was real—she stumbled a little, and I grabbed her arm to keep her from falling.

"Try to get some sleep," Kathleen said gently.

"I appreciate the sentiment, but we both know that's not going to happen," Annie replied.

"Pat, will you stay with her tonight?" our big sister asked me.

"I'll be there as long as she wants me."

"Good. Now if you two will excuse me, I need to get back to work. I'll drop by the store in the morning and bring you up to speed."

"Thanks. That's greatly appreciated. See you then," I said, and then Annie and I made our way back to our vehicles. "Did you really just stumble? Are you okay?"

"As much as I can be," she said. "Come on. Let's go. I'll see you at the Iron in a few minutes."

CHAPTER 4: ANNIE

I GOT TO THE IRON PARKING lot just behind Pat, and he climbed into my Subaru after he parked his truck off to one side. It was way too early to be out and about in Maple Crest, but I couldn't imagine going back to sleep after what had just happened to Timothy. The town was filled with darkness, with only a few dots of light coming from scattered streetlights as we drove beneath them. As I kept driving toward Robin's place, I saw lights on in one house, coming from the kitchen. Lester Pender was up late, if he'd even gone to bed yet. Lester had complained to me a few times at the grill about his insomnia, but I hadn't really believed him. The lights emanating from his kitchen were more convincing than anything he could have said face to face.

"It appears that we're not the only ones awake," Pat said as he pointed to Lester's house.

"Do you mean besides all of the volunteer firemen and police still at Timothy's cabin?" I asked.

"Does anyone *volunteer* with the police force?" Pat asked me.

"You know what I mean. I still can't get over what happened tonight."

"It can be a dark world out there, can't it? And before you say anything, I'm not talking about the time of day or the lack of sunshine at the moment."

"I suppose if I were to think about it rationally, I wouldn't be all that surprised that something like this could happen here," I said as I drove on. "After all, I see it on the news all of the time. People literally die every day in tragic ways."

"True, but this is personal. We knew Timothy, and now he's gone," Pat answered after a moment of silence. "It really brings it home."

"We both know that he was more than just a passing acquaintance to me," I reminded my brother, as though I even had to.

"As callous as it might sound, I'm just glad that you two weren't still dating," Pat said. "This would have been ten times harder on you."

"I'm not even sure about that. It's pretty tough to take as it is. I realize that Timothy wasn't the love of my life, though there was a time I suspected that he might be, but it still crushes me to know that now there won't ever be a chance for the two of us to get back together again."

Pat looked at me with surprise. "Was there ever any real possibility of that happening before he died?"

I thought about it for a few moments before I spoke. "No, probably not. Being dumped on the front porch of the Iron in front of my brother was pretty final for me. It's always been tough for me to go back once I've been tossed away."

"Me, too," Pat said.

It was my turn to look surprised at him. "Even with Molly?" The two of them had a seesaw past, but they'd always ended up back together, and a part of me thought that they still might.

"No, never with Molly. She's the exception," Pat said. With a hint of hesitation in his voice, he admitted, "The truth of the matter is that I've been fighting the impulse to call her again." My twin said it as though he'd just confessed to a much worse crime than missing his ex-girlfriend.

"Mmm."

"That's it?" Pat asked as he glanced at me. "That's the only reaction I'm going to get from you? Why aren't you trying to talk me out of it?"

"Patrick, I know better than to do that. You're going to do what you want to do, and no amount of advice from me is going to change that. In many ways, you're more stubborn than I am."

"You don't honestly believe that, do you?" he asked me with a grin.

"I refuse to answer that," I said. "Besides, there's no time; we're here." I looked at the dark house and knew that we were about to ruin someone else's night. I was definitely having second thoughts about waking Timothy's assistant up. "Are you sure we shouldn't give her a few hours of sleep before we wake her up and ruin what's left of her night?"

"Annie, I understand why you're asking, but we need to do this before our big sister gets around to it. If she gets to Robin first, what are the odds that she's going to talk to us at all?"

"That's a good point," I said as I parked the car and shut off the engine.

As we approached Robin Jenkins's front door, the porch light sprang into life. "Is it possible that she's already up?" Pat asked.

"I bet that light has a motion detector," I said as I rang the bell.

Robin answered the door after the second ring, and from the state of her hair and the puffiness around her eyes, it appeared that we had indeed awoken her. "Pat? Annie? What are you two doing here? Do you know what time it is?"

Unfortunately, I was well aware of it. "I'm sorry. We wouldn't be here if it weren't important. May we come in?"

"I suppose so," she said as she cinched her robe tighter around her waist and stepped aside so we could come in. To me, Robin was pleasingly plump, though I knew some men preferred their women bony and thin. These weren't men I cared to associate with myself, since I too carried a few more pounds than I technically should have. Robin had been pretty in high school, but that had begun to fade, and I wondered if she ever regretted the boys she'd cast aside back then. I knew there were a few I wished I could get another shot with now that I'd grown up. As a whole, they'd all been just a little too nice for me at the time, and now it constantly amazed me how I ever could have considered that a flaw in someone.

"What's going on?" she asked.

"It's Timothy," I said without delay. "I'm afraid he's dead."

"No. That can't be," she said numbly, and then Pat caught her just before she hit the floor.

Robin had fainted from the news, and I had to wonder if there had been more between her and her former employer than just a job.

"Put her on the couch," I ordered Pat.

"I can do that," he said, his voice straining under the exertion. Once he had her there, I went into the kitchen and drew a glass of water. There was a variety of knickknacks around, and I noticed with some amusement that they were all horses. It appeared that Robin had an affinity for equines, from the potholders to the salt and pepper shakers to the cast iron horses scattered everywhere. Even the glass I used to draw water featured a rather content pony winking at me.

"You're not going to throw that on her, are you?" Pat asked me when I returned with the full glass.

"Of course not. I thought a few sips might help her when she comes to."

"A little booze might be better," he said.

"Do you happen to have any on you, because I didn't see any in the kitchen," I replied.

He was saved from answering when I heard Robin shift a little. "What happened?" she asked, and then a cloud came back across her face. "It's true, isn't it? Timothy really is dead."

"I'm so sorry," I said as I offered her the water. She sat up, took a few sips, and then she handed the glass back to me.

"Thank you. What happened? Did Jenna kill him?"

Pat looked shocked by the question. "Not that we know of. Why would your mind go straight to something like that?"

"Pat, it was getting clearer every day that Jenna and Timothy did not belong together. These last few weeks, all they've *done* is argue. Was he poisoned? Since she's a veterinarian, I'll bet she has access to all kinds of deadly things."

Was Robin actually considering the possibility? I needed to tell her what had happened. "No, he died in a fire. I'm afraid he didn't have a chance."

"Oh, no. His beautiful cabin. It's gone too, isn't it?" Robin looked as though she were about to break down, but she somehow managed to pull it together again. "Why didn't the police come and tell me what happened? I wasn't just his employee; I was his best friend, too."

"I'm sure they'll be along soon," I said, "but we were wondering if Timothy had problems lately with anyone in his life, personal or professional. Besides Jenna, I mean," I quickly added.

I watched as Robin bit her lower lip, and then she took another long sip of water before she spoke again. "I'm not sure I should talk out of turn."

"Robin, I cared for Timothy, too. You know that, don't you?" I asked her, doing my best not to start crying myself.

She looked at me hesitantly before she trusted herself to speak. "I do. I don't know what he was thinking dumping you for Jenna. You were much better for him than she ever was. As a matter of fact, anyone would have been."

Including you? I asked silently to myself. I wasn't at all sure that Timothy had even been aware of his assistant's feelings for him, but they were crystal clear to me, especially now that she was so vulnerable. Had she been secretly hoping that someday he'd realize that she was right under his nose? If she had, that hope was now gone forever. "We just want to find whoever is responsible for this and make sure they pay for what they've done," I said.

"I understand. I know you two have solved murders before. Timothy was always quite impressed with your track record. In fact, I'm sure that if he were able to communicate with us now, he'd approve of your investigation."

I wasn't at all sure of that myself, but I wasn't about to dispute it, and I hoped that my brother would keep his opinions to himself as well. "Thank you. That means a great deal to both of us. Any help you could give us would be greatly appreciated. Thoughts?"

"If I were to start digging into our client list, I'd have to start with Gordon Freeman. Timothy was getting ready to drop him as a client, but Gordon wasn't having it. He threatened Timothy a few days ago, if you can believe it."

"What does Gordon do?" I asked. I'd seen the man around town some, but I knew that he didn't live in Maple Crest.

"He has a dry-cleaning shop over in Pepper's Landing, but Timothy was beginning to suspect that he was laundering more than clothes."

"Like money, perhaps?" Pat asked her.

"What else? He's got some rough connections, so it wouldn't surprise me."

Gordon would certainly bear looking into. "Anyone else?" I asked.

"Do you mean clients? I'd say that Viv Masters would have to go on your list. She's been making passes at Timothy for months, but lately she's gotten nasty about his constant refusals."

"I know Viv," I said. "She runs First Cut." First Cut was a newer hair salon trying to get a foothold in town. Viv was a brassy woman with high hair and tight clothes, and pity the person who sat down in her chair who might be allergic to perfume. Viv believed that if a little was good, a lot was better. "I had no idea. Are there any other folks we should check out?"

"Not clients that come to mind, but I'd talk to his brother, if I were you."

"Mick? What about him?" I asked. I knew Timothy had an older brother, but they had been estranged for as long as I'd known him. "I didn't think they spoke."

"They didn't, at least until their father died last month. Mick accused Timothy of cheating him out of his rightful share, which Mick considered to be three fourths of everything. His dad made Timothy, the younger son, his executor, because he knew better than to trust Mick with the responsibility, and it was a point of contention between them that kept escalating. Hey, I wonder if Timothy's death impacts how their father's money was distributed. Could Mick get it all now that his brother is gone?"

"I don't know, but it merits investigating," I said. "Do you know where we can find him?"

"Didn't you know? He's been in town for the past week," Robin said. "I thought you two were aware of everything that went on in Maple Crest."

"Clearly we aren't. Do you know where he's staying?"

"He's boarding with Louisa Holliday and Cynthia Blakely."

"So, they're finally making good on their threat to open a bed and breakfast," I said. The pair of older widows was constantly coming up with schemes to supplement their meager retirement incomes, but I was surprised that they'd finally committed to something.

"Mick's their first paying guest, from what I understand. He's been complaining about the lack of service there, but they're cheaper than the worst motel on the edge of town, and that's really all that he cares about. He definitely should go on your list."

"We'll talk to him," I said. "Anyone else?"

"Not off the top of my head, but if I think of anyone, I'll let you know. Will you two excuse me now? I need some time to process what's just happened. I still can't believe that he's gone."

"Neither can we," I said. "Call us if you think of anything else that might be helpful."

I grabbed Pat's arm and led him out.

"Wow, can you believe she gave us so many names?" my twin asked me as we walked back to my car.

"Knowing Robin, I'm not all that surprised. You know, we need to put her on our list as well."

Pat looked shocked by the suggestion. "Seriously? Why would she kill Timothy?"

"You know she was in love with him, right?" Had my brother missed that detail? He was usually pretty savvy about that kind of thing, but he had his own set of blind spots, just like the rest of us.

"You're kidding."

"Not even a little," I said. "If she decided to declare her love for him and he rejected her, I could see Robin killing him and burning his place to the ground."

"I'm having a hard time grasping that," Pat said.

"That's because you don't realize what we women can be capable of, especially when we're scorned by those we love."

"Wow, I'm beginning to think that maybe I should have been a little more careful when I broke up with my girlfriends in the past."

"Don't worry; I think you're safe. So, what should we do?"

"There's not really anything else we can do at this hour. Let's go back to the Iron," Pat suggested.

I glanced at the clock on my dash. "I don't know about you, but there is no way I'm opening the store this early."

"I wasn't suggesting it. I thought a nap might be in order."

"That's fine for you, but where am I supposed to sleep?" I'd bunked with my brother before, but his couch wasn't all that comfortable. Still, it would be better than going home and smelling that smoke again. It was an aroma I hoped that I never had to endure again.

"Tell you what. You take the bed, I'll take the couch," he said. "We can't exactly go knocking on any more doors at this time of night, and besides, we still have to open the Iron this morning. If we can nap now, we'll be in better shape to tackle our list of suspects once we close the place for the day."

"I can't believe you're suggesting we should open for business as though nothing has happened," I told him.

"Annie, no matter what, we still need to make a living, and shutting the store and grill down won't bring Timothy back. Besides, you know the Iron is the hottest spot in town for gossip. I say we go about our day, but we keep our eyes and our ears open. We might just get lucky if we do that."

"Okay, I can see your point," I reluctantly agreed. "You don't have to give up your bed, though. I can handle the couch for a few hours."

"Nonsense. I insist," Pat said.

"Okay, then. I accept."

He grinned at me before he spoke. "You didn't really put up much of a fight."

"What can I say? I'm just trying to be a good guest," I answered with a slight smile of my own. Leave it to my brother to be able to bring a little bit of light into the darkness my world had become.

———————◦◦◦◦◦◦◦———————

He'd been right after all.

A few hours of rest made all of the difference in the world. By the time we were ready to open the Iron, we were both more than capable of tackling the world, and as soon as we locked our doors for the day, we'd start our investigation.

———————◦◦◦◦◦◦◦———————

It turned out that we didn't even have to wait that long to do it, though.

CHAPTER 5: PAT

"**J**ENNA, WHAT ARE YOU DOING here?" I asked my ex-girlfriend as I unlocked the door to the Iron so we could open for business. Annie was already back at the grill making homemade bread for the day, while I'd taken care of the front part of our place, which was a general mercantile. A small post office occupied a little of our space as well. It was tight, but we made it work.

"Seriously, Pat? I thought we'd gotten past all that. You know as well as I do that there's nowhere else for me to shop. Maple Crest isn't all that big."

"I'm fine with you coming in, but given what happened this morning, I didn't think shopping would be very high on your list of priorities."

"What are you talking about?" Jenna asked me. She was clearly confused by my comment. Was it possible she didn't know what had happened to her boyfriend?

"You don't know, do you?"

"I don't have any idea what you're talking about, but if it happened around here last night or this morning, I wouldn't know. I was with my sister in Hickory all night. Timothy and I had another fight. This one was a blowout. It's over, Pat. I realize now that I never should have left you for him. It was a mistake I'll regret for the rest of my life."

"Jenna, something happened to Timothy." I didn't know how to tell her that he was gone.

Her face went ashen. "He didn't try to hurt himself, did he? I knew he'd take the breakup hard, but seriously? Is he in the hospital?"

"I'm afraid he's dead," I said.

Jenna looked at me as though I'd suddenly started speaking Latin. "What? That's impossible. I just spoke with him yesterday. We were supposed to go out to dinner, but I knew I couldn't sit through a meal with him knowing that I was about to end our relationship. We had it out once and for all at his cabin, and then I drove straight to my sister's place. You must be mistaken."

"I'm afraid there's no doubt about it," I said, but as I did, I had to wonder, was Kathleen really that certain the body they'd found belonged to Timothy? From what she'd told us, he'd been burned beyond recognition. How long would it take to find his dental records and compare them with the teeth they'd found at the site? "His cabin burned down, and he died in the fire." There was no sense in making matters worse by telling her that my older sister suspected that it was from foul play.

"I don't believe it," she said stonily as Annie approached us. My twin sister must have noticed that I was talking with Jenna, and she'd made her way up front, abandoning her bread for the moment.

"Jenna, did Pat tell you about Timothy?" Annie asked her.

"It's true, then?" she asked me haltingly.

"I'm so sorry," Annie said, and then my sister did an amazing thing. Putting their past differences aside, she hugged Jenna tightly as my ex-girlfriend began to cry. I should have offered her comfort myself, but Annie was better in those situations than I'd ever been. As she was consoling her, Annie mouthed the words, "Call Kathleen" to me. Had she made the gesture to keep Jenna there, or was there a dual purpose to the offer of sympathy? It didn't matter. I did as she suggested.

Stepping away from them for a moment, I dialed Kathleen's number.

She answered impatiently, "Patrick, I haven't had enough time to come to any conclusions yet. These things take as long as they take. I'll call you when I know something."

"Don't hang up," I said. I knew that she'd been about to, based on my past experience with my older sister. "Jenna is here."

"Jenna Lance? At the Iron?"

"Yes," I said softly. "Annie's comforting her at the moment. We just told her what happened to Timothy."

After a moment's pause, Kathleen said, "I really wish you had let me do that."

"Sorry, but I wasn't thinking of you at the moment. I'm not sure how long we'll be able to keep her here, though. I just thought you'd like to know that she was back in town."

"Back? Where was she?" Kathleen asked, though I could hear she was multitasking as a car engine roared to life in the background. Evidently she was going to talk and drive at the same time.

"She told us she had a fight with Timothy yesterday. She broke up with him, as a matter of fact, and then she headed straight for her sister's place in Hickory."

I thought I'd been circumspect, but when I looked up, Jenna was staring at me. "Is that your sister on the phone?" she asked me.

"I thought you might like to talk to her about Timothy, since she knows more about what happened than we do," I explained quickly. It would have been the nice thing to do, even if it hadn't been my primary motivation for calling Kathleen.

"Let me talk to her," Jenna demanded as she reached for my phone.

"She wants to talk to you," I told Kathleen before Jenna ripped it from my hand.

"Where are you? I need to know about Timothy right now." After nodding a few times, she said, "Okay." As Jenna handed my cell phone back to me, she said, "She's on her way. Thanks for calling her, Pat."

"Sure," I said, feeling uneasy about getting praise for doing something for my sister's benefit and not hers. "Glad to help."

Thirty seconds later, a squad car came tearing into our parking lot. Kathleen got out and hurried for the door, where the three of us were waiting for her.

"I need to know everything," Jenna said.

Kathleen nodded toward us, and then she turned to Jenna. "I understand, but we shouldn't do it here. Pat and Annie are just opening for the day, and there's going to be a crowd of customers here soon." I appreciated her optimism, but I doubted we'd be experiencing any sudden morning rushes. "Let's go back to my office where we won't be disturbed."

"I don't care where we do it," she said. "I just want to know what's going on."

"Come on then," Kathleen said. "Thanks for the call, Pat," she added before they left the Iron together.

Annie looked at me after they were gone and asked, "Was that a good idea, calling Kathleen so quickly?"

"I don't know, sis, it was yours. What choice did we have? Jenna has to be high on Kathleen's list of suspects. It would have been negligent of us not to tell her that she was with us."

"I know. That's what I was thinking when I suggested it, but now that Jenna is gone, I'm beginning to wonder. Pat, do you believe her?"

"Which part?" I asked.

"That she broke up with him. After all, the only other person who can refute it is conveniently dead."

"Annie, what could it possibly matter *who* ended things?" What was my sister driving at? Even as I asked myself the question, the answer popped into my head. "You think if he broke things off with her, she might have killed him in a fit of rage, don't you?"

"It's a possibility that we need to consider," my sister said. "Whether we like it or not, Jenna is smack dab in the middle of this murder investigation."

"I still have a hard time believing she could do something like that," I said, realizing that Annie was right. No matter how illogical it might seem on a rational level, I knew that rage could do terrible things to someone's judgment, no matter how levelheaded they might normally be.

"I know. I'm sorry, there's no way around it. We have to consider the possibility that Jenna killed Timothy." She looked as upset saying it as I was hearing it.

"Okay. If Jenna did kill him, it's probably going to be on Kathleen's shoulders to prove it. We need to spend our time trying to figure out if any of our other suspects might have done it instead."

"We certainly have a list to choose from," Annie said as a timer went off in back. "That's my bread," she said, rushing to the grill part of our business.

"Relax, it just went off," I said as I followed her to the back. I was stopped short by Edith, our mail lady, and Skip, our young assistant, as they walked into the Iron together.

"Sorry we're late," Edith said. "It was all my fault. I had a flat tire, and Skip was kind enough to change it for me."

"I was happy to do it," the young man said. "I can't believe what happened to Timothy Roberts. How's Annie taking it?"

"She's pretty upset," I said, trying not to give too much away about our decision to investigate on our own.

"I imagine she would be," Edith said. "I'll go see if I can offer some comfort to the poor child."

I knew that Annie wouldn't want to be fawned over, no matter how good Edith's intentions might be. "I'm sure she would appreciate the gesture, but let's all give her a little space right now, if you don't mind," I said softly.

"Yes, you're right. That would be for the best. Tell her I asked about her, would you?"

"Me, too," Skip added.

"I will, but the best thing we can all do right now is to go about our normal duties and give her time to let it all sink in."

"Very good," Edith said. Before she disappeared into her own domain, the small corner of the space that served as the mail drop for our town, she patted Skip on the cheek gently. "You're a fine young man, and I appreciate you very much. I don't know what I would have done if you hadn't come along when you did and rescued me."

He blushed slightly under the praise. "Anybody would have done it."

"Tell that to the four cars that passed me by before you stopped," she said, and then she did as I suggested and entered her mailroom domain.

"What can I do this morning?" Skip asked me.

"Well, first you can wash your hands," I said as I looked at the grease stains covering his fingers and palms.

"Consider it done," he said with a grin. "And after that?"

"We got a shipment in yesterday of Christmas decorations. Why don't you carve out room for a display?"

"I'd love to. Could I add a few of my own things into the mix?" Skip was constantly trying to find a way to make extra money using his many talents, and I had no problem with him displaying the crafty pieces he created.

"What did you have in mind?"

"Let me show you," he said as he dug into his letter carrier bag and pulled out a five-inch decorated Christmas tree cut from a thin piece of veneer. It even sported tiny painted lights and garlands on it. "I've got lots more. What do you think?"

"This one is great," I said. "How are you going to display them, though? They are ornaments, aren't they?"

"Well, they are now," he said with a grin. "All I need to do is drill a hole through the star on top and put some thin red ribbon through it. That's brilliant, Pat."

"I'm glad I could help," I said. "I'm curious, though. What was your original plan?"

"I made little bases with slots in them," he explained as he dug out a small two-inch-by-four-inch piece of wood painted white. Skip had cut a slot in the top, and after setting the base down on a nearby counter, he stood the tree up as a three-dimensional display. "Ta da. I won't need the bases now, though, since I'm making these into ornaments."

"Don't do anything rash," I said. "Sell them both ways. You could have some trees on stands and others as ornaments. You know, I think you may have something here. Have you thought about making snowmen as well?"

Skip frowned for a second, and then he broke out into a grin. "Cool. I can make a longer base and have snowmen and Christmas trees placed randomly. Man, you're contributing so much to this project I feel as though I should cut you in on the profits."

Coming from Skip, I knew what a concession that would be. "Thanks, but just make me three sets for myself and we'll call it even."

"Sure thing, but why three?" he asked me.

"I'm going to need one set for me, and one each for Annie and Kathleen. I've been wondering what to give them for Christmas, and these would be perfect."

"Done and done, boss," he said. "Now I'll get busy on that display."

"After you wash up," I reminded him.

"Check."

CHAPTER 6: ANNIE

I GOT TO THE BREAD JUST as it was about to burn on top, which was a real relief, since I'd already invested so much time in it. I'd been experimenting lately with baking my bread in a cast iron Dutch oven, and so far, I'd been loving the results. At first it seemed counterintuitive to put the dough in a closed container after it had risen, but I was a true believer after I realized that the bread steamed as it baked. During the last five to ten minutes, I removed the lid and let it brown naturally until it developed a crisp crust to go with the moist interior. After it cooled, when the bread was cut, it felt more like a sourdough variety than a plain yeast bread recipe, with holes and pockets of air scattered throughout the loaves. I'd snuck down to the kitchen a few hours earlier to get it started since I was staying with Pat, and I'd mixed up the dough so I could give it enough time to rise before I baked it.

I was just slicing one loaf up for French toast when I saw someone approach my counter. Pat wouldn't have known him on sight, and he must have walked right past my brother without him realizing who it was.

Unfortunately, the two of us had met before.

"Hello, Mick. Sorry for your loss," I said automatically.

"You're not surprised I'm in town, Annie? Is this place really that big a gossip mill?" he asked with a frown. Mick had been quite a bit thinner when we'd first met, but he'd since packed on the pounds in all of the wrong places. When I'd been dating his little brother, Timothy had told me that Mick went through wives like some men traded in cars. He had a habit of marrying eighteen-year-old girls, no matter his own age. The last I'd heard, his fourth and hopefully final wife had left him, no doubt in search of a man and not a petulant little boy. Mick's looks had faded over time, and I doubted he could snare another teen in his trap, though I doubted it would ever stop him from trying.

"What can I say? News travels fast in a small town," I said. "How long have you been here?" It was a question I'd been dying to ask him, and I was ready with it when he'd suddenly showed up.

"I've been here a few days," he admitted. "Timmy and I have been wrangling about our father's estate, since he was in charge. I don't know what Dad was thinking. Maybe he felt sorry for him."

I knew that Timothy hated being called Timmy, and the only one who did it was his older brother. While Timothy had gone on to college, getting a degree in accounting and making something of himself, his brother had tried to skate his way through life. For some reason, their father had indulged his older son, bailing him out of trouble again and again, but now Mick's safety net was gone. "I didn't realize your father had passed away," I said. "It's been a pretty tough time for you, hasn't it?"

"It would have been easier if Timmy had loosened up the purse strings. I asked for a reasonable advance against my inheritance, but he wouldn't give me a nickel. Instead, he kept pushing off the final disposition until the last minute. I don't know what I'm going to do now that he's dead. I'm probably going to have to hire a lawyer to sort this mess out."

"I'm sorry his death is going to be such an inconvenience for you," I said, slamming a cup down in front of him and filling it quickly with coffee, managing to splash a little on his hand in the process. It had been difficult to do intentionally, but I'd somehow pulled it off, and for some odd reason, I was proud of the fact.

"Hey, that's hot," he protested.

I tossed him a dishrag. "So sorry. What can I get you?"

"How about some burn ointment?" Mick asked as he dabbed at his hand.

I looked at it a second, and then I shook my head. "You know, if you hadn't moved the cup, it wouldn't have happened." It was true that he'd touched it, though barely, and it had had no impact on my aim, but I was going to head off a lawsuit before he could even consider it.

"Whatever," he said, the resignation clear in his voice. "What's good here?"

"Everything," I said. "I thought you were staying with Louisa and Cynthia at their B&B. Doesn't that, by its definition, include breakfast?"

"If you can call it that. The only thing they had to eat this morning was oatmeal. I hate oatmeal."

"Well, you're in luck. I've got other choices. What can I get you?"

"What's the special? Anything cheap?"

I wanted to take the dishrag from him and smack him with it, but I resisted the temptation. "I'm making French toast with homemade bread," I said.

After I quoted him the reduced price, he grimaced a little before saying, "I suppose that would be okay."

"Well, I've always got the Twofer. It's even cheaper."

He showed a little interest. "What's that?"

"Two eggs and two pieces of toast," I said with a smile.

"No sausage or bacon?" he asked.

"Sure, but that would be extra." For some reason, I loved giving this man bad news.

"You know what? I think I'll pass on all of it." As he stood, he reached for his wallet, but I figured that since I'd splashed him with the coffee, it wouldn't be right to charge him for it.

"Don't worry about it. It's on the house."

"Why? Because you burned me, or because my brother just died?"

"Let's say it's in honor of your brother's memory and leave it at that," I said, meaning it as I said it.

"Is it too late to change my order, then?" Mick asked me with what he must have thought was a charming smile.

It didn't work on me. "Yes. Have a good day."

Mick frowned at my refusal, and then he walked out of the Iron, a little the worse for wear.

Pat joined me in back as I was wiping up the spilled coffee. "What was that all about, Annie?"

"You two have never met. That was Timothy's older brother, Mick," I explained.

"As he walked past me, he said something about suing us, but the place wouldn't be worth it if they gave him the keys."

"Ignore him. He's a whiney little baby," I said.

"Is it true? Did you splash him with hot coffee on purpose?" Pat asked me.

"Not nearly enough of it, if you ask me," I admitted. "He's more upset about their father's will being held up than he is about Timothy's death."

"What are you talking about?" Pat asked me.

"Evidently Timothy was the executor, even though he's younger than Mick, and he's been dragging his feet settling the estate. That's why Mick said that he was in town. He admitted that he and his brother have been battling over the will since he arrived."

Pat took that in. "That gives him a motive then, doesn't it?"

I considered it for a moment before replying. "Pat, I can't stand the man, but would he kill his last remaining family just for money?"

"I don't know him at all. You tell me," Pat said.

Once I looked at it in those cold and calculating terms, I realized that it could be true. "It's possible. He admitted that they've been arguing about money since he arrived. Do you think he's trying to do a preemptive strike by announcing it to any and all who will listen to him?"

"I don't know what to think, but Kathleen needs to know what's going on with Timothy's brother. Are you going to call her, since you're the one who just spoke to Mick?"

"I suppose I have to," I said. "Hey, you didn't have much of a breakfast. I know you were worried about Jenna, but at least she showed up. Can I whip you up some French toast?"

"I really shouldn't," he said, though it was clear by his tone of voice that he wanted to.

"Come on, Pat, live a little. The store's not crowded, Skip can handle anything that comes up, and you deserve something good to eat."

"Okay, you twisted my arm," he said with the hint of a smile. "Make it quick though, okay? I don't like taking Skip off his display work."

"Seriously? Christmas decorations already?" I asked as I dipped slices of my handmade bread into the batter I'd prepared.

"You're kidding, right? Halloween will be here before we know it, then Thanksgiving and Christmas will steamroll overtop of us if we aren't ready for it."

"I suppose, but it seems to come earlier and earlier every year," I said.

"What can I say? The world is losing its patience with the natural order of things," Pat said as I poured him some coffee.

I made myself a few slices as well, and my brother and I ate our meal together, one on each side of the counter. We were barely finished when the front door opened and five different people came into the Iron. Three headed for the mercantile, and two walked straight toward my grill. Pat shoved his plate away as he stood. "Thanks. That was awesome."

"I appreciate the praise," I said. "I'll call Kathleen later, okay? There's no real rush, since Mick isn't going anywhere until he gets his hands on his father's money. I wonder who Timothy left his money and his land to."

"I don't know, but I have a feeling we're going to find out."

"I just hope it wasn't me," I said as I cleared away our plates.

Pat looked surprised by my statement. "Is that even a possibility?"

"No. Of course not. I'm just saying, I don't need folks around here to have any more reasons to suspect me of being involved in what happened to him than they already think they do."

"I understand that," Pat said. "Just call her when you get a chance, okay?"

"Yes, sir, I'll get right on that," I answered with a mock salute.

Pat just shrugged and went back up front. I'd call Kathleen during the next lull, but at the moment, I had orders to fill and customers to serve.

Oddly enough, I managed not to spill anything hot on any of them. Would wonders never cease?

———————————

I got a break a little later and called my big sister, for all of the good it did me.

"Kathleen, did you know that Mick and Timothy were fighting about their father's estate over the past couple of days?"

"I did. How did you hear about it?" she asked me.

"Mick came by the grill earlier," I admitted.

"I heard all about it," she said dryly. "Annie, did you really scald his hand with coffee? And if you did, was it an accident, or did you do it on purpose?" My sister clearly disapproved of my actions.

"Would I do something like that on purpose?" I asked her, being as insincere as I knew how to be. "Besides, it was just a little splash. If I'd been meaning to scald him, I would have poured the whole carafe straight into his lap."

"Remind me never to get on your bad side when you've got a pot of hot coffee in your hands," Kathleen said.

"Oh, I think we both know you're too smart for that. Seriously though, he's got to be a suspect in your mind, doesn't he?"

"Annie, it's only natural for you to want to know what happened to your ex-boyfriend, but I'm handling it, okay?"

I decided my best course of action was not to answer the question at all.

She waited two more beats before asking me, "Annie? Are you still there?"

"I am," I said.

"You didn't answer my question," Kathleen said flatly.

"Sorry, but I've got to go. I've got a crowd coming in, so I need both hands free." The "crowd" was Cora Yount, and she was all alone.

Could I help it if I was in no hurry to anger my sister, who also happened to be our sheriff?

CHAPTER 7: PAT

A S EXPECTED, TIMOTHY WAS JUST about all folks could talk about at the Iron. I must have answered a thousand questions about what I thought, and I was certain that Annie had gotten the same treatment working the grill.

An hour before we were set to close for the day, crusty old Virgil Hicks came in carrying a plastic bag with our store logo on it. "I need to return this, Pat."

I took the bag from him and looked inside. "It's the dog whistle you bought a few days ago," I said. "What was the problem with it?"

"It didn't work," Virgil said with a frown.

"You know humans can't hear it, right?"

He looked at me as though I had the IQ of a banana. "I'm not an idiot. It didn't work on the dog it was supposed to."

"Virgil, when did you even get a dog?" I couldn't help myself asking. It had been an odd purchase for him to make in the first place, but more than that, I was just relieved not to be fielding another question about Timothy Roberts.

"It's not for my dog."

"Whose dog was it for, then?"

"Are you going to give me a refund or not?" Virgil asked me.

The man was a real grump, and ordinarily I wouldn't have pushed him on it, but I wasn't in the mood to be confronted in my own store. In other words, Virgil had chosen the wrong day to come looking for a fight. "Whose dog?" I repeated my question.

"Beatrice Masterson's. Are you satisfied?"

"She's your next-door neighbor, isn't she?" It was all starting to make sense now. "Virgil, you have to get pretty close for this whistle to work."

"I don't care anymore. I'm done trying to get that mutt to stop barking at night."

I couldn't even imagine how frustrating that must be for him. "No worries. Sorry. I'll take care of it right now."

Virgil looked surprised by my sudden turnaround. "That's it? No more third degree?"

"No, we're good," I said as I offered him a smile. I took Virgil's receipt, entered it into the register, and then I gave him his cash back. "There you go."

"Okay then," he said as he took the money, sounding a little deflated. It seemed as though he'd been looking forward to digging in his heels, and I'd disappointed him somehow.

"Was there anything else?"

"I might look around a little," he said.

I waved to the store. "Go ahead and knock yourself out."

As Virgil browsed, I started straightening up the checkout counter. It was amazing how quickly things got out of sorts, and I found myself constantly reorganizing the impulse items we offered at the front. Summers were the worst when the kids were out of school, but there was always something that needed doing throughout the year. I didn't even notice as Virgil approached and put some dog jerky treats on the counter.

"If you can't beat them, join them. Is that it?" I asked him with a grin.

Virgil shrugged. "Who knows? Maybe these will do the trick. I figure if I throw one over the fence at night, that fleabag will shut up long enough for me to get to sleep. After I'm out, a freight train wouldn't wake me up."

"You know, you could always just say something to Beatrice," I said as I rang up the new sale.

"We don't talk," he said abruptly.

I was amused to see that the amount of jerky he'd purchased was more expensive than the whistle he'd just returned, so we were coming out ahead of the game after all. "At all?"

"That's right. You haven't heard what happened? I was mowing my lawn two years ago, minding my own business, when a wasp flew in my face and stung me straight on the nose. I lost control of the mower for a second and got two of her plants, and you'd think I'd painted her house purple. I offered to buy her two replacements, but she kept screaming at me that they were priceless. Pat, they were annuals! How could they have been priceless? We haven't spoken since."

"You know how Beatrice feels about her flowers. She's been running the Ladies' Floral Society for as long as I can remember. They're like her children."

"Then she should have put that fence up *before* I mowed her kiddies down," Virgil said with a snap. Was he actually blaming her for not doing a better job of protecting her flowerbeds from his errant lawn mower? If it had been anyone else, I might have believed it was hyperbole, but knowing Virgil, I had a hunch he was deadly serious.

I didn't know how to respond to that without poking him again, and I'd suddenly lost my taste for a fight. "Thanks for shopping at the Iron. Come again."

The only problem was that Virgil wasn't finished. "It was a real shame about Timothy Roberts," he said, watching me for some kind of reaction as he lingered at the counter.

I wasn't about to fall into that trap. "It sure was."

Virgil smiled softly. "I wonder if the cops are looking at Viv Masters."

That got my attention, since Viv was already on our list. "I'm sure Kathleen is looking at everyone who might have had a reason to harm Timothy. Why do you think Viv might be one of them?"

"The way those two were around each other? If your older sister isn't looking at her, then we've got the wrong person acting as sheriff in these parts."

"What are you talking about?"

"Two days ago," Virgil said, warming up. "I was walking down the street when I saw them run into each other in broad daylight."

"Were they fighting?"

"No, they seemed civil enough to me," Virgil said.

"Then what was the problem?" Was the man so bored with his life that he was just making things up now?

"After they said their good-byes, I happened to glance back at Viv. You should have seen the look she gave him! It could have melted the flesh right off the man! I've never seen such pure hatred in my life, and I don't have to tell you that I've been around the block a time or two."

Was he exaggerating again, or had he really seen something? With Virgil, it was always hard to tell. "Do you have any idea why she was upset with him?"

"Upset? It was more than just being upset," Virgil said. "Pat, I'm telling you, she wanted his head on a stake."

It was pretty clear that Virgil didn't know any of the details. "You should tell Kathleen what you saw," I prompted him.

He looked surprised by my suggestion. "Why would I get myself involved in that mess? She's supposed to be such a great cop, let her figure it out on her own." Virgil shook the bag of jerky treats at me, and then he left the Iron. I thought about calling Kathleen and telling her what he had said, but then I had second thoughts. Viv was already high on our list, and Annie and I would be talking to her soon. Why muddy the waters by telling Kathleen before we had a chance to find out if Virgil had an overactive imagination, or if he'd really seen something between the two of them? If we suspected that Viv was hiding something after we spoke to her, we'd tell our sister, but first we needed to do a little preliminary work ourselves.

Still, it gave me food for thought as I continued to wait on our clientele.

I was just locking the front door when I saw a police squad car pull into our lot. In less than a minute, Kathleen herself was approaching.

"I guess I was just hoping that it was all some big mix-up, that somehow it wasn't Timothy after all," Annie said.

"I understand that."

"How did he die, exactly?" I asked. "Was it from the fire?" I hated myself for asking, especially since Annie was clearly feeling so vulnerable at the moment, but Kathleen was willing to talk, and we might not be so lucky if we waited to ask about it later.

"No, as a matter of fact, it was the smoke that got him," she said.

I couldn't imagine what that might mean, and I wasn't going to ask Kathleen with Annie sitting close by.

Annie frowned for a moment when she heard the news. "If it was smoke related, why didn't he just leave the cabin before he died?"

It was a fair question, one I'd thought of as well, but not something I was going to ask. That didn't mean that I wasn't glad that Annie had.

"We found him locked in the closet off the living room," Kathleen said.

"How do you know the door was locked if everything burned up?" Annie asked her.

"The door burned to a crisp, but the knob was metal. The mechanism was in the locked position. I'm sorry to have to tell you this, but I wanted you to hear it from me first."

"So, there's no doubt that it was murder, then," I said.

"Not in my mind, unless he happened to lock himself in his own closet by accident at the same moment a fire started. That's too big a coincidence for me to swallow."

"I agree," I said.

Kathleen stood, and Annie and I joined her on our feet. "Anyway, that's why I came by. I wanted you to hear it from me first."

I knew that I had to tell her what we were up to, and not just because she was our sister. As sheriff, she had a right to know that Annie and I were going to dig into this. "Kathleen, we're not going to stand on the sidelines. You know that, don't you?"

Our older sister frowned a moment before she spoke. "I've got this

47

under control, and I don't need the two of you going around stirring up trouble."

"I'm sorry that's the way you feel," Annie said calmly, "but there are things Pat and I can do, questions we can ask, that you can't. Let us help you. Please." The choking in her voice was real; I knew that my twin sister was being sincere, and what was more, I had a hunch Kathleen knew it as well.

"You both must realize that I can't officially sanction anything," she said after a few moments of thought. "So if you want to ask some questions and nose around a little, you'll have to do it without any official approval from me. Do we understand each other?"

"Thank you," I said as I started to hug her.

She backed up a step. "Hang on; I'm not finished. If you find anything of value, and I mean anything, you come straight to me with it. Agreed?"

"Of course," Annie said, but I wasn't so ready to concur.

"What if we don't know if it's important, or at least not right away? I can't imagine you'd be interested in hearing about every wild theory and each dead end we go down."

"No, I don't have time for that," she agreed. "Okay, I'll be reasonable about it just this once, given the circumstances. You don't have to share anything with me until you're certain that it has something to do with what happened to Timothy. Don't abuse my good nature. Understood?"

"Completely," I said. She'd just given us enough leeway so I wouldn't have to disclose our list of suspects or what Virgil Hicks had shared with me earlier. Annie and I had no real evidence at that point. Everything we believed was based on speculation, a secondhand eyewitness, and our knowledge of the key players in the case. I knew well enough that the pass she'd just given us wouldn't cover everything we might find, but it was a good place to start.

"Well, we won't keep you," I told Kathleen as I started walking her up to the front of the Iron. "I know you've got a lot going on right now."

Annie stayed behind to clean up from our early dinner, but Kathleen followed me, and as I began to close the door behind her, she said softly, "Look out for her, do you hear me?"

"I always do," I said. "Thanks. It helps not feeling so powerless about everything."

"Just be careful. Both of you."

"You can count on it," I said.

Kathleen smiled softly at me before she answered. "Pat, if I could believe that, I'd sleep better at night, but we both know that's not about to happen."

I grinned in return. "You know us too well," I said. "Happy hunting, sis."

"You, too," she said, and then she was gone.

CHAPTER 8: ANNIE

"WHAT WAS THAT ALL ABOUT?" I asked my brother as soon as our older sister was gone. I'd seen the two of them whispering about something, and it made me think of a saying I'd once heard: Just because you were paranoid didn't mean that they *weren't* out to get you.

"What are you talking about?"

"Your little chat with Kathleen," I asked him.

"She's worried about how you're handling all of this," Pat confessed. "To be honest with you, so am I."

I felt like a heel, jumping to conclusions that they'd been somehow conspiring against me. "I'm sorry. I guess it's still sinking in. The thought of him being trapped in that closet and the smoke coming in through the cracks is killing me."

Pat put his hands on my shoulders. "So don't think about it."

"Sure. Okay. Sounds good. Any advice on exactly how I should go about that?"

"Hey, I'm good at giving the advice. How you apply it to your life is up to you." He offered a soft smile, one that I returned. "How much time do you need to finish up here?"

"Give me ten minutes. Does that work for you?" We'd already sent Skip home, and Edith was off by then anyway.

"That's perfect. I need to balance the books, get the deposit ready, and then we can go. Want to race?"

"What are we, twelve?" I asked him.

"You're right."

"No, I mean I'm all for it. Ready, set, go!"

I worked furiously getting the kitchen and grill back in good shape, but I didn't cut any corners. It wasn't worth winning just to have to come back the next day and redo something.

At least I didn't think it was.

I noticed that Pat was done with his chores before I'd finished mine, but he was clearly dragging his feet in order to let me be first. Did I need a win that badly? I did not. "Hey, if you let me win, you have to do dishes back here for a month."

Pat grinned at me as he answered, "Well, would you look at that? I just finished."

"Good for you." After my last tasks were completed, I joined him up front. "Let's go. I take it we're stopping off at the bank on our way, right?"

"You know me too well. I hate having too much money around here at any one time."

"Then let's do it," I said.

When we got to the bank, Pat asked me, "Do you want to come in with me?"

"I thought you used the night drop," I said.

"I usually do, but I have to check on something inside, too."

"There isn't a problem with our account, is there?" I asked him. The last thing I needed to deal with at the moment was a business-related emergency.

"No, it's nothing like that. I'm just running low on deposit slips, so I thought I'd order more."

Was that true, or was there another reason Pat wanted to go in and handle things personally? I took a wild stab and asked, "It doesn't have anything to do with the new teller, does it? What's her name, Clarise?"

"It's Carly," he supplied automatically, and then he caught on to what I'd just done. "You think you're so smart, don't you?"

"I have my moments. Don't mind me. Take all the time you need. She's cute."

"I'm sure I don't know what you're talking about," Pat said, a little louder than he'd needed to.

"Sorry. It must have all just been in my imagination."

Pat didn't comment, but I could have sworn I caught a smile as he stepped inside the bank.

I was still considering the possibility that my brother was finally moving on from Jenna when I saw someone approaching from behind.

It was Robin Jenkins.

"You must be so relieved," she said excitedly.

I had a feeling she wasn't talking about the way Timothy had perished. No one could get excited about that. "I'm not sure if I am or not. What's going on?"

"You should know better than anyone else. Your sister arrested Jenna Lance this morning," she said smugly.

"What? When did this happen?" I couldn't believe Kathleen would arrest anyone, especially Jenna, without telling us about it first.

Robin looked confused. "She took her out of the Iron in her squad car, from what I heard. Weren't you there?"

It suddenly all made sense. "Robin, Jenna asked Kathleen for details about what happened to Timothy, and my sister offered to tell her back at her office. I'm not sure who told you that she was under arrest, but I can assure you that wasn't the case, at least it wasn't when she left the Iron this morning."

Robin looked disappointed by the news. "Oh. I suppose that makes sense. Sorry. I must have gotten my facts wrong. Where was she when Timothy died, though? I for one would like to know the answer to that."

"According to what she told us, she was at her sister's place," I said, immediately regretting it. I wasn't exactly sure that fact was mine to share. I hoped that if it got back to Kathleen, she'd be in a forgiving mood.

"Oh. Okay. Thanks for clearing that up. Do you have any idea who your sister might suspect?" Robin asked me.

"I'm certain she's still gathering information," I said. "These things take time."

"Well, I know she hasn't talked to me yet. Wouldn't I be the logical choice to interview, given my close relationship with Timothy?"

"Don't worry, I'm sure she'll get around to you soon."

"I certainly hope so," Robin said, and then her cell phone rang. "Hello? Yes. Of course. Three minutes. Yes. Good-bye." She looked at me smugly as she said, "Speak of the devil and he appears, or she, as it is in this case. Your sister would like me to come down to the sheriff's office and have a chat about Timothy."

As she turned to go, I asked, "What about your banking?"

"It can wait," Robin said as she waved a hand in the direction of the bank. "This is important."

I wondered who was about to get tarred next as I watched her drive hurriedly away.

"Was that Robin Jenkins I just saw you speaking with?"

I nodded as my brother rejoined me. "She thought Kathleen arrested Jenna this morning."

Pat frowned before he spoke. "Why would she think that?"

"Evidently someone saw them leave the Iron together and leapt to the wrong conclusion."

"People in this town gossip too much," my brother complained.

I looked hard at my brother before I replied. "Pat, are you still carrying a torch for Jenna?"

"What? No! Of course not! I just don't think it's right that some folks are dragging her name through the mud without cause, you know?"

"Oh, there's a *little* cause," I said.

"I thought you'd forgiven her about the breakup," Pat said to me.

"I've done my best to, but forgetting is an entirely different matter. How's Carly doing? Did you get all of your banking done?"

"Yeah, but she was on break," he said before pursing his lips slightly. "Did Robin stop by just to tell you about Jenna?"

"No, she was heading inside the bank when Kathleen called her. That woman was absolutely tickled to be going to visit the sheriff."

"It's probably not as sinister as all of that. Maybe she just wants her boss's killer caught," Pat said. He looked around the parking lot, and I wondered if he was searching for Carly.

"Looking for someone special?" I asked him.

"No, I thought I heard someone cough."

Okay, if that was his story, I wasn't going to challenge him on it. "If the banking is taken care of, who's first on our list?"

"Take your pick. If we want to start close to home, we should speak with Viv Masters at her hair salon. On the other hand, if you feel like a drive, let's go track Gordon Freeman down in Pepper's Landing."

"What about our other suspects?" I asked him.

"Let's see. You just spoke with Robin, and I have a hunch she's going to be tied up with Kathleen for quite a while, given her propensity to gab. As for Mick, I don't want to brace him until we have something substantial we can call him out on."

"He had *plenty* of incentive to get rid of his little brother, if you ask me," I told Pat. "That man is up to something; you mark my words."

"Consider them marked," Pat said with the hint of a grin. "Should we flip a coin? Would that help you decide?"

"There's no need to," I said. "Let's go talk to Viv first. There are several things I'd like to discuss with her about her relationship with Timothy."

"Do you think she's going to be all that interested in speaking with us?"

"Why shouldn't she be?" I asked him.

"Annie, you were Timothy's girlfriend for quite a while. Don't you think she might have resented that fact if she were secretly in love with him?"

"That remains to be seen, but you're forgetting something. I'm old news. If Jenna was trying to get information out of Viv, I have a hunch that she'd be out of luck, but I plan on playing the 'woman scorned' card with Viv. We'll see if she was personally invested in Timothy or not by the time I'm through with her."

———— ✦❦✦ ————

"Hey, Viv, do you have a second?" I asked the hair salon operator when my brother and I walked into her shop. I had a hunch that she did, since the three chairs in the place were all empty. Betsy and Polly, her two employees, were cleaning, while Viv sat in one of the chairs reading. Viv was a little older than Pat and I were, but the years hadn't been quite so kind to her. Heavy makeup covered her face, and her hair had been dyed so many different colors over the years that I doubted she remembered the original shade she'd been born with. She was thin to the point of being bony, and she had an air of a woman stuck out of time. No doubt Viv would have been better suited for the 1960s, and she wasn't all that happy that they had passed her by.

"I could probably squeeze you in if you want a quick cut and style," she said as she studied my hair. "I was wondering when you'd get around to changing it."

I touched my hair defensively. "Why, what's wrong with it?"

"Annie, it's a little young for you, wouldn't you say?"

I wasn't in any mood to debate my hairstyle choices, certainly not with a woman who wore her hair teased to the sky and sprayed with enough hairspray to keep it from ruffling in a hurricane. "We're not here about my hair, Viv."

"That's why I'm here with her," Pat said. Though Viv had ignored him, Polly and Betsy had both noticed my brother's presence instantly. Betsy had just gone through a nasty divorce, and Polly was notorious for being on the prowl searching for her first husband. I started to worry about bringing Pat with me, but I knew my brother could handle himself. Besides, he usually was oblivious to the attention most women paid him; even Jenna had taken a while. I suspected it was because he'd given his heart to Molly a long time ago, and he'd never quite gotten over it. Why couldn't they work things out? The entire town knew that they belonged together; if only we could convince them of that.

"I just assumed you were keeping her company," Viv said. "What is it you wanted to discuss with me?"

I glanced at the other women, who were watching us openly as we spoke. "Could we step outside, maybe? It's such a beautiful day, I hate to be inside one second more than I have to."

Say what you would about Viv, but she wasn't slow in picking up my intention. "That's a good idea." She then turned to her staff and said, "Ladies, I'll be right outside. Hold down the fort."

"We can do that," Polly said, and then she smiled brightly at my brother. "See you later, Pat."

"Me, too," Betsy added quickly, not to be outdone by her coworker.

"Sure thing," Pat said, clearly confused by their attention. I thought about sitting him down and having a talk with him, but I'd promised not to meddle in his love life, and so far, I'd kept my word, no matter how hard it was to hold my tongue at times.

Once we were outside, Viv turned on both of us, and her usual smile was gone. "This is about Timothy, isn't it?"

"We just need to clear a few things up with you," I said, trying to keep my voice as cheerful as I could manage. "Were you in love with him, Viv?" I hadn't planned on coming right out and asking her, but what better way to get to the heart of the matter than by the direct route?

"What? No. Of course not." Her protest might have sounded real enough if it hadn't been for her delay in answering. "Where did you hear such nonsense?"

"From more than one source, actually," Pat said.

"Name them."

"Viv, we're not going to tell you what other people said any more than we would repeat anything you might tell us. You can trust us." It was true, as far as it went, unless it turned out that she had killed Timothy.

If that were the case, all bets were off.

"What of it? We flirted back and forth, but nothing ever came of it. I don't know why folks don't realize that's just the way I am. I flirt with every man I see."

"Funny, but you've never flirted with me," my brother said.

Viv smiled at him and patted his cheek gently. "My dear boy, how would you even know? You miss more signals than a blind semaphore operator."

Pat frowned, but before he could protest, I decided to steer the conversation back to the point. "Viv, we heard that you were getting fed up with Timothy's rejections, and you have to admit, you have quite a temper at times."

"I won't apologize for it. I'm passionate, like every true artist is," she said. "And if one of you say that what I do isn't art, then this conversation is over."

We both decided to stay silent, which was a good plan if we wanted to ask her any more questions. "The truth of the matter is that someone saw you staring Timothy Roberts down so hard on the street the other day that they were amazed his head didn't burst into flames," I said.

Viv frowned for a slight second, and then she laughed. "I don't even have to ask you who that was. Virgil is quite the gossip, isn't he? They say women are bad, but older men are the worst. If Virgil doesn't find drama around him, he does his best to create it. As usual, he was overexaggerating. Timothy said something about my new fragrance being a little too potent for his taste, and I defended my choice. It meant nothing to either one of us. I was his client, and he was my accountant. If something had happened to my shampoo supplier, would you have come to speak with me, too? I doubt it, unless you dated him as well, Annie. Did you, by any chance? I'd like a little warning next time if something untoward happens to Phil."

"No, I didn't date your shampoo supplier," I said, fighting to keep from blowing up. "Timothy and I weren't going out anymore either, remember?"

"Certainly, but since he and Jenna were on the outs, who knows? He may have come running back to you at any moment. Now that you've lost that chance, I can understand why you're both so gung-ho about finding out what really happened to him. If you truly want to corner someone with a motive, you should speak with Gordon Freeman from Pepper's Landing. I walked in on the two of them arguing about something last week, and it wasn't pretty."

"No worry there, he made our list," Pat said, and I wanted to kick my brother. The less information we gave any of our suspects about what we were up to, the better, at least as far as I was concerned.

"Good. And there's always Robin, his assistant. The woman was a walking cliché, falling for her boss like that. She must have not enjoyed being constantly passed over so many times."

"Viv, as much as we appreciate your input, we'd really like to talk about you. Do you happen to have an alibi for last night, say between midnight and two a.m.?"

Viv frowned at me for a moment before speaking. "I was alone, if that's what you're asking, so no, I don't have anyone who can verify it. Why, can you supply one of your own? Whether you like it or not, your name should be on your sister's list of suspects, too."

"I was alone as well," I said.

"Then you'll have as much trouble proving it as I will," she said. "Now, if you two will excuse me, I've got things to do inside."

I couldn't imagine what they might be, but it was clear we weren't going to be getting anything else out of her at the moment. "Fine. I'm sure we'll be talking again," I said.

"You know where to find me," Viv said, and then she walked back inside.

"Do you believe her?" Pat asked me as soon as she was gone.

"What, her alibi? Who knows? She's right about that. It's going to be tough for me to prove, too."

"I'm talking about the way she felt about Timothy," Pat replied.

"No. Not for a second. Does Viv strike you as the type of woman who takes no for an answer?"

"Not really," Pat said. "We've done all that we can here. Let's go speak with Gordon."

"Somehow I don't think it's going to be any better than this was," I said.

"Cheer up, sis. That's why we make the big bucks."

"You know we aren't getting paid for this, right?" I asked him with a grin.

"It was a figure of speech," he said as we got into my car and headed for Pepper's Landing to speak with someone else who might have had something to do with my ex-boyfriend's death.

CHAPTER 9: PAT

"WHAT DID VIV MEAN BACK there?" I asked my sister as she drove us to the nearby town. She would ride around in my truck if we weren't going very far, but any distance at all and she preferred her transportation to mine.

"Which part?" Annie asked me, keeping her eyes on the road, though traffic was so light we nearly had the highway to ourselves.

"About me being oblivious to women flirting with me," I asked. "Is it true?"

"Do you want the short answer, or the long one?"

"The short one," I said.

"Yes."

I glanced over at my sister and saw that she was smiling at me. "Annie, I'd like something a little more detailed than that."

"I think it's charming that you barely notice when a woman throws herself at you. You have no inkling most times, do you?"

"What can I say? I'm a friendly guy. I like chatting with people, and when they interact with me, I'm just enjoying the conversation."

"There's your problem," Annie said.

"Explain."

"You show interest in them as people, and some of them think it's because they are women."

That thought hadn't even occurred to me before. "But they are people and women, too. Can't they be both at the same time?"

"Yes, but you've got to remember, there are some women who take any sign of attention from a man as meaning that he's interested in them. I don't mean me, but some women."

I pondered that a few moments before speaking again. "So, I guess I really am dense when it comes to that sort of thing."

Annie smiled at me and risked a quick glance in my direction. "Don't change a thing about the way you are, brother dear. It's one of the things that makes you so loveable."

"Was Timothy like that, too?" I asked her.

She bit her lower lip before answering. "Yes, it was a trait the two of you shared."

"If Viv was actively flirting with him, and he basically ignored her or didn't see the signals, could that make her angry enough to kill him?"

Annie hesitated again before replying. "Most women would just write it off, but Viv has always seemed like the type of woman who would hold a grudge. If he caught her in the wrong mood and said something that set her off, it's possible. For her it could have been a matter of pride."

I shook my head, not following the logic at all. "I just don't understand women, Annie."

"That's okay. As much as we'd like to think we're different, we usually don't understand you, either. There's the town limits sign."

I looked up to see the sign proclaiming that we were welcome in Pepper's Landing. What kind of name was that, anyway? To my knowledge, there wasn't another place nearby named Salt's Pier. I took little consolation in the fact that today appeared to be one of those days were nothing made sense. I had them, but rarely, something I was extremely thankful for. Most times, the world around me made perfect sense; there was more order than chaos in my life, and the sun rose in the east and set in the west.

Today, I wouldn't be sure until I saw the sunset. It was just that kind of day.

As we drove through the small downtown area, I realized it could be just about anywhere in the South. Along the way, I noticed a barbeque joint, a chain grocery, a pair of competing gas stations, more churches than you could shake a stick at, and several storefronts with soaped-up front windows. The downtown looked as though it was struggling to hang on, and I found myself rooting for it. There were enough strip malls in the world; I liked the charm of a true downtown and hoped they'd find a way to bring it back.

"Hang on a second," I said as Annie started to approach the dry cleaner's that Gordon owned. He was standing out front, and a car slowed down as it neared him. I watched as the window rolled down, and Gordon handed what looked like a stuffed business envelope through the open window. The driver barely slowed down for the exchange, and a moment later, he took off as though he were late for dinner.

"What was that all about?" I asked Annie as she drove closer.

"I'm not sure, but I don't think we should mention it unless the opportunity arises. Why don't we stick with Timothy as our topic for now?"

"Sounds good to me," I said. "Do you want to take the lead, or should I?"

"Why don't you do most of the talking, and I'll chime in if it's appropriate?" my twin sister asked.

"Why not, since that's what you're going to do anyway," I said with a grin.

She didn't take offense, as I knew she wouldn't. After all, why should the truth bother her?

"Pull over there. I'd love to corner him before he gets back inside," I said.

Annie did as I asked, and as Gordon was nearing the door to his place, I called out, "Hang on a second. We'd like a word with you."

He turned and looked at us, and then he glanced back to where the other car had so recently been. When he made sure they were gone, he shrugged and stopped until Annie and I could both get out and approach him.

"You're both a ways from home, aren't you? I thought you never left your store and grill."

"As a matter of fact, we get out all the time," I said. "Right now, we're tracking down folks who saw Timothy before he died. We understand you spoke with him yesterday. If you don't mind us asking, what were you so upset about?"

"Who said we were upset?" Gordon asked me. It was pretty obvious that he was doing everything in his power not to glare at my sister and me.

"Does it really matter *where* we heard it?" Annie asked him. "What was the fight about? Was he really dropping you as a client? That must have made you furious."

"Is that what his snooping assistant told you? As a matter of fact, I was firing *him*. I didn't like the way he was handling my books, and there was no way I was going through another tax season with him as my accountant. He tried to talk me out of leaving, but I told him that my mind was made up. I don't know why Robin would say otherwise."

"We aren't confirming or denying we heard anything from her. You understand that, don't you?" I asked him, not wanting to get Timothy's assistant in trouble with this hotheaded man because of us.

"Sure, if it wasn't her, maybe a little bird told you instead. I don't care where you heard it. It's wrong. I fired him, not the other way around. I pay my bills on time, I run a legitimate business, and I'm not hard to work with. What possible reason would he have for getting rid of me?"

He was baiting us, trying to see how much we knew or had just seen. I hoped Annie would stay quiet. We might need the information to use against him later, so now was one of those times where discretion really was the better part of valor.

Thankfully, my sister didn't say a word.

When Gordon saw that we weren't going to comment, he added, "I had no reason to wish ill of the man, no matter what you or anyone else might think. Is that all?"

It wasn't, not by a long shot, but I had a hunch that if I was going to ask him any more questions, I'd better be quick about it. "Do you happen to have an alibi between midnight and two a.m. this morning? We're asking everyone," I said as nonchalantly as I could.

"I don't have to answer that. I'm finished with the two of you." With that, he turned and started to walk inside his dry cleaner's.

"Were you alone, or were you with someone?" I pushed him as he started to disappear inside.

"That's none of your business," he barked at me, and then he was gone.

"Should we follow him in?" Annie asked. "We didn't ask him about what we just witnessed."

"I'm glad you followed my lead," I said. "Let's save that in case we need it later."

Annie looked at me closely before she spoke. "You're not afraid of him, are you?"

"Him, no, but his connections? We'd be crazy not to move cautiously, Annie. I have a hunch his business partners wouldn't like us digging into his life."

"Then we'll have to watch our step, won't we?" my sister asked.

"It wouldn't be a bad idea. Where should we go now?"

She looked around Pepper's Landing. "There's nothing here for us. Why don't we head back to Maple Crest and see what's going on there? Maybe we can find a little more trouble to get into before the day is done."

"You know, I wouldn't be the least bit surprised," I said, and she started driving us back.

As Annie drove toward Maple Crest, she said, "Pat, I'm going to suggest something that I'm pretty sure you aren't going to like."

"Then why not save yourself the trouble and not say it at all?"

"Sure, I can do that," she said, and for the next two minutes, we rode in silence.

It was a game that I knew I was going to lose. I held out as long as I could, and then I finally asked her, "Fine. I give in. What is it?"

"I didn't think you wanted to hear it," she said. "I respect your wishes, Pat. It's okay."

Her reasonableness just served to drive me crazier. "I was wrong, okay? We should consider every idea at this point."

"We need to go see Jenna," she said.

"No."

"No? That's it? Discussion closed?" Annie asked me. "If you're uncomfortable doing it, that's fine. I'll drop you off at the Iron, and then I'll go see her by myself, but like it or not, we need to talk to her. She's hip deep in this case, and we can't just ignore her."

"You're right," I said softly.

"I mean, I get why you wouldn't want to talk to your former girlfriend, but you've got to be reasonable, Pat."

"In case you didn't notice, I just agreed with you," I said the moment she took a breath.

Annie glanced over at me. "I thought I just heard you say something, but I couldn't believe my ears. Brother dear, did you just say that I was right?"

"I won't repeat it," I said with a gentle smile. "Let's go see what we can find out from Jenna."

"I'm proud of you," Annie said as she patted my knee gently. There was no sarcasm in her voice, something that was a relief to me. My sister knew all of my buttons, so the fact that she refrained so often from pressing them was entirely to her credit.

"You would have done the same thing if our roles had been reversed," I told her.

"I'd like to think you're right, but I can't be positive. If you'd like, I'll take the lead with her this time."

"No, we can do it together, just like always," I said as I tried my best to get used to the idea of questioning Jenna. Annie was right, but that didn't mean that I had to like it. I'd done my best to avoid having any prolonged conversations with her since she'd dumped me for Timothy, and now I was about to go out of my way to talk to her. That was just one of the prices we paid for digging into crimes without any authorization. Sometimes it meant we had to do some pretty distasteful things in the course of our investigations.

———◦⟨◦⟩◦———

As we neared Jenna's house, I saw black smoke coming from the back. "Is that another fire?" I asked Annie as she pulled into the driveway. "I'm calling 911!"

"Hold on," my sister said as she put a hand on my arm. "That's clearly not a house fire."

"How can you tell? It might have just gotten started."

"Pat, let's take thirty seconds and check it out first, okay?"

"Fine," I said, "but I'm going to call it in if anything looks suspicious at all." We got out of her car and raced to the backyard. I was expecting to see Jenna's porch on fire, but instead, she was sitting near a sheet-metal fire pit, burning what looked like notes and receipts. "Thank goodness," I said as we approached her.

Jenna must not have heard us coming, because she looked positively startled at the sound of my voice. "Pat. Annie. What are you two doing here?"

I was about to tell her that we wanted to ask her some questions when my sister had an even better plan. "We were driving by and saw smoke. After what happened to Timothy, we were afraid that the arsonist had struck again."

I had to hand it to Annie; it was a brilliant cover story that explained our presence without giving away the fact that we were there to interrogate her.

"No, it was a cool day, so I thought I'd get rid of some old paperwork I've been holding onto from the vet clinic."

"We have recycling, you know, and if those documents are too sensitive, there's always a shredding service," Annie said.

"I never trusted them," she said. "I've thought about getting a new shredder after my old one conked out, but I figured I could burn these until I could order one."

"Okay," I said, shuddering a little at the thought of having an outdoor fire so soon after Timothy's place had burned to the ground. "Jenna, do you have a second?"

She poked at the flames with an iron, and I saw curls of paper ignite upon fresh exposure to the fire. "I guess so. I'm not going anywhere. What's up?"

"You said you were at your sister's place in Hickory when Timothy died, right?" Annie asked her.

"That's right. I just can't prove it at the moment."

"What do you mean?" I asked her.

"She went out of town as soon as I came back, and evidently she left her cell phone at home, because Kathleen told me that she's not answering her calls."

"Isn't it unusual for someone to travel without their phone these days?" Annie asked her.

"You clearly don't know my sister. She'd forget her head if it weren't attached. Anyway, she'll be back in a few weeks, and Kathleen will be able to confirm my alibi then."

"Jenna, I know it must be painful for you, but do you know of anyone who might have wanted harm to befall Timothy?" Annie asked her gently.

"That's all I've been able to think about since I found out that it happened," she answered. "Timothy didn't like to talk about work, so if it were someone related to his accounting practice, I wouldn't know about it. As for his personal life, well, that was mostly just me. Sorry, I can't help."

"What about his brother, Mick?" I asked her. "Did he ever say anything about him?"

"Oh, yes. Timothy wasn't a fan, and that's putting it mildly. Apparently, when they were growing up, Mick had done his best to make Timothy's life miserable. Some of the things he did would land him in jail today, but his parents just ignored his behavior. Do you want an example? As a joke, he used to squirt Timothy with lighter fluid and then flick matches at him. If you ask me, he was a real monster."

"That's terrible," I said. I found it hard to believe that a sibling could act that way toward another one. Kathleen, Annie, and I had battled through many differences over the years, but there had always been a core of love there that outweighed everything else. What a miserable existence Timothy must have gone through growing up. It was a wonder it hadn't scarred him for life, but clearly he'd found a way to get past it all. I hadn't liked everything that the man had done in his life, especially when it related to my twin sister, but all in all, I'd liked him.

"That's not the half of it. I could tell you stories that would curl your toes. Mick being back in town brought up a lot of old memories that Timothy had tried to repress. If I were you, I'd speak with the man."

"We have," I said.

"Then I'd do it again. Timothy tried his best to be fair with Mick about their father's estate, despite all that had happened between them in the past, but Mick expected nothing less than the lion's share of everything as some kind of birthright just for being the eldest son. What a waste of oxygen."

I couldn't blame Jenna for feeling that way about Timothy's brother. I knew that Annie had heard a few stories herself, but nothing like she must have been made aware of.

"We'll talk to him again," Annie said. "What about Robin?"

Jenna shrugged. "It's an old story, isn't it? She was secretly in love with Timothy, but he thought of her more like a little sister. I knew that it killed her inside whenever she saw us together, so I tried to downplay our relationship whenever she was around."

"Could she have killed him?" I asked her.

Jenna looked startled by the idea. "I don't know. There's a great deal going on behind those eyes. Maybe. I don't know; right now I seem to be jumping at shadows."

"What's that?" Annie asked suddenly as she pointed toward the fire. "That looks like a greeting card."

"Oh, I tossed in a few old pieces of mine to keep the fire going," Jenna said, and then she took the poker and moved the burning papers around until the card was obliterated by flames.

"Gotcha," Annie said.

Jenna's cell phone rang, and after she checked the number, she said, "Sorry, but I've got to take this. One of Hannah Lee's guinea pigs has a cold again, and she's worried sick about her. Luna is prone to infections, and that girl loves her critters more than some folks care for their children. Not that I can blame her; they're cute little rascals, full of all kinds of personality quirks."

As she took the call, Annie and I waved good-bye and headed back to my sister's car.

"Did you see that card?" my sister asked me once we were back inside.

"No, I wouldn't even have noticed it if you hadn't spotted it. What did it say?"

"I couldn't tell," she replied, "but I could swear something was written on it in Timothy's handwriting. Wouldn't she want a keepsake of her dead love? Why burn it the day his body was found?"

"Maybe it's too painful for her to keep around," I suggested.

"Maybe," Annie said with a frown.

It was a good thing she was paying more attention to her driving than she was to me.

Somebody suddenly jumped out in front of her car, and if Annie hadn't been alert, we might have had another fatality in Maple Crest within twenty-four hours of the last one.

CHAPTER 10: ANNIE

I COULDN'T BELIEVE IT WHEN ROBIN Jenkins jumped in front of my Subaru. Luckily I wasn't looking at Pat at the time, or things might have ended very differently. I slammed on my brakes, and then I rolled down my window. "Have you lost your mind? I could have killed you!"

"Somebody's following me!" Robin said, nearly out of breath as she kept glancing behind her. "You've got to help me!"

I pulled the car off to the side of the road, parked it, and then Pat and I got out. We both looked up and down the residential road, but no one was in sight. "I don't see anyone," Pat said.

"I'm telling you, they were there!" Robin was clearly distraught, but was it because of her imagination, or had someone really been following her? "It's the truth. You've got to believe me!"

"Settle down," I told her, lowering my voice and hoping that she'd catch a little of my calmness. "Take a deep breath, and then tell us all about it."

Robin took several breaths before she spoke again, and I was glad to see that she finally managed to calm herself down. "Sorry. It's just really unsettling."

"Tell us exactly what happened," Pat said gently.

"I was out for my evening walk—it's something I do every night, rain or shine—when I had a feeling that someone was following me. I tried to glance back over my shoulder to see if anyone was there, but they were too fast for me, and I never caught sight of them. I heard their footsteps, though, and when I went around a corner, they sped up."

Pat said, "Hang on a second. Which direction were you coming from when you flagged us down?"

"I was coming from back that way," she said as she pointed over her shoulder, toward Jenna's place.

"I'll be right back," Pat said as he strode off in that direction.

"Do you want me to come with you?" I asked him.

"No. Stay here with Robin." He must have seen the dour expression on my face, because he quickly added, "If you don't mind."

"No, I'm happy to do it," I said, trying to sound cheerier than I felt.

Two minutes later, Pat rejoined us. "Whoever was back there is gone now." I was glad he'd phrased it that way. It gave some credibility to Robin's story, and I was certain that it made her feel as though we believed her.

I wasn't sure how Pat felt, but the jury was still out as far as I was concerned. Still, if someone had been following her, it was reason enough to be so upset. I tried to put myself in her shoes and knew that I would have been rattled, too, given the circumstances.

"Robin, do you have any idea *why* someone would be following you?" I asked her.

"It has to have something to do with what happened to Timothy, don't you think? Why else would someone want to stalk me? I bet this ties in with what I saw at the office this afternoon."

"What are you talking about?" I asked her.

"I happened to glance out the window just before I left, and I could swear I saw someone lurking in the bushes. Not only that, but when I went outside to see, whoever it was disappeared! As if that weren't bad enough, I got ready to leave, but then I realized that I'd left my lunch bag in the kitchenette. I went in to get it, and while I was back there, I noticed a few things that needed to be thrown out of the fridge. By the time I took care of that, I was walking back out front when I heard someone trying the door handle. I yelled and told them we were closed but that I'd be right there, but by the time I unlocked the door and opened it, whoever had been there was gone." Robin took a deep breath, and then she studied my brother and then me a moment before speaking again. "I know how this sounds. You two must think I'm crazy."

"We realize this is a stressful time for you," Pat said, which wasn't the most politic way of putting it.

"I swear, I didn't imagine it. Someone tested that door trying to get in, and now they are following me around town. What could they possibly want of me? I don't have any evidence about who killed my boss."

"Maybe they think you know something that even you aren't aware of," I said.

I thought the reinforcement of the idea that she wasn't crazy would be helpful, but it simply set off a completely different wave of paranoia in her. "They're out to get me now? Am I being set up as the next victim? Should I ask your sister for police protection? I don't know anything! I swear it!"

Everything we'd done to try to calm her down was now wasted. If anything, she was more frantic than she had been before. "Robin, would you like a ride home?" I offered her.

"No. I want to go straight to the police station!"

It was clearly an order, not a request. I didn't just want to show up there and catch Kathleen off guard. "Let me call my sister and tell her we're coming."

Pat frowned, but I had no idea what part of our plan of action he wasn't happy with.

Robin seemed to have immediate second thoughts about approaching Kathleen. "I've changed my mind. I want to go home."

"That's probably for the best," my brother said calmly.

"I just can't face being interrogated by anyone right now," Robin said as she got into the back seat of my Subaru. At least it was relatively clean back there.

As Pat and I drove her home, Robin got more and more antsy in back. When we pulled up to her place, I decided to offer our assistance again. "Are you sure you'll feel comfortable going inside alone now?" I asked her.

"Could you both possibly come in and check under the beds and in the closets for me?" Robin asked meekly. "It's the only way I'm ever going to be able to get any sleep tonight."

"We'll be glad to," I said, and then I turned to my brother, who was frowning at me. "Right, Pat?"

"It sounds like a plan to me," he said with a shrug.

As we got out and followed Robin to her front door, Pat tugged on my arm and asked softly, "Annie, what exactly are we going to do if someone is lurking inside? It's not as though either one of us is armed with anything more than an angry look."

"Do you honestly believe we're going to find anyone inside?" I asked him.

"No, I'm just asking what our plans are if we do."

"We all scream and run away," I said with a shrug. "I don't know what to tell you." What did he want from me? I wasn't about to start carrying a handgun around in my purse, and a baseball bat wouldn't fit. I liked our chances anyway, since I didn't think we'd find anything untoward inside.

Pat and I searched through every room in the house, with Robin close on our heels the entire way. Once she was satisfied that no one was lurking in the shadows, it was as though I could see a weight being lifted off her shoulders. "Thank you both for doing this."

"We were happy to," Pat said, "but if you see anything else tonight, you really should call the sheriff."

"I know. I will. I just couldn't face her tonight. There's just one more thing you could do for me, if you wouldn't mind."

Pat looked as though he were about to refuse her request when I stepped in. "What can we do to ease your mind further?"

"Go by Timothy's office and make sure everything there is okay. Would you do that for me?"

"I'm not sure that we should, at least not without a police officer," I said.

Pat nodded in agreement. There was only so far we could allow ourselves to be pushed, and Robin had already exceeded the limit.

"Please? If it's nothing, no one else but the two of you will know how foolish I've been if I'm wrong."

"And if you're right?" I asked her.

"Feel free to call your sister. This is ridiculous. I'm jumping at shadows everywhere I look. I'm telling you, I can't stay in this town a moment longer. As soon as the sheriff gives me permission, I'm getting out of Maple Crest, and I'm never coming back. My sister in Virginia has been asking me to move up there for ages, and this is as good a time as any, since I'm out of a job *and* a killer might be after me. Would you go check on the office right now for me? I can't bear the thought of someone desecrating Timothy's space."

"We'll check it out for you," I said as Pat started shaking his head, ready to refuse her request, no doubt.

The moment we were outside, I heard the deadbolt lock click into place. Apparently Robin wasn't taking any chances.

"Seriously? How much are we expected to indulge that woman?" my brother asked me. "She's taking advantage of our good natures. The sheriff should be dealing with her fears, not us."

"Pat, you saw how frazzled she was," I explained. "Do you honestly think that throwing her together with Kathleen right now is a good idea? She's ready to cut and run as it is. What can it hurt for us to swing by Timothy's office and make sure everything is fine over there?"

"None, I suppose," Pat answered. "Is there a chance in the world we're going to find anything out of order there, either?"

"I doubt it. Why else do you think I was so willing to check it out?"

———— ✦✦✦ ————

It turned out that we were both wrong, though.

When we got to Timothy's office, we noticed two things that didn't make any sense.

The lights were on inside, and the front door was ajar.

That never could have happened if Robin had closed the office properly. Had she left in such a rush that she'd forgotten to turn off the lights or even close the door behind her, or had someone come along behind her and broken in?

The real question was if someone else had been there, were they gone now, or were they still inside, looking for something we didn't know was there?

———✦✧✦———

I grabbed my cell phone and dialed my sister's phone number, just in case we needed her.

It went straight to voicemail.

"She isn't picking up. Now what do we do?" I asked.

"I guess we could always call 911," Pat suggested.

We were still trying to decide what to do when we saw the front door open, and Mick Roberts stepped outside, holding a thick file folder in his hand.

———✦✧✦———

"What do we do now?" I asked Pat, but I was talking to empty air.

My brother had already jumped out of my car and was hurrying toward Mick.

I had no choice but to follow.

What had we just gotten ourselves into?

CHAPTER 11: PAT

"S TOP RIGHT THERE," I COMMANDED. Darkness had fallen swiftly around us, sending the world from light into shadow in the short span of time it had taken us to drive from Robin's home to Timothy's former office.

Mick Roberts did as he was told. "Don't shoot!" he yelled as he raised his hands in the air.

Annie joined me, and we approached Timothy's brother side by side, coming close to a streetlight as we did so. "We weren't about to do anything that rash. What do you think you're doing, Mick?" I asked him.

He looked relieved to see that it was just us, though if he'd known us at all, he might not have been so relaxed about our presence there. "This was my brother's office. I have every right to be there."

"I'm not so sure about that," Annie said. "Do you have the sheriff's permission?"

"How did you even get in?" I asked quickly as a follow-up. "I doubt Timothy gave you a key." After hearing the story of their childhood, I was surprised Timothy had ever spoken to the man again. Knowing him though, he'd probably done it out of a sense of obligation to his late father, though I doubted that would have been reason enough for me if I'd been in his shoes.

"The door was already open and the lights were on," he said. I wondered about that, especially given Robin's story, but there was really no way to prove it one way or the other. "It can't be breaking and entering if I didn't break anything going inside."

Apparently Annie wanted to wipe the smug look off his face. "How about unlawful entry or trespassing?"

That threat got his attention. "Since neither one of you is a cop, I don't care what it *might* be."

"Call Kathleen again," I directed my sister.

Annie hit redial, and this time, the sheriff picked up immediately. My sister turned on the speakerphone feature so I could hear as well. "What is it, Annie? I kind of have my hands full at the moment. There was a hit-and-run on the edge of town, and we're canvassing the neighborhoods looking for a dented fender with red paint on it."

"Was anybody hurt or killed?" I asked.

"Is that Pat? Am I on speaker? You know I hate that."

"Sorry," Annie said, but she made no move to change the setting. "What happened?"

"Nobody's hurt. It's property damage only. What's up?"

"We just found Mick Roberts leaving Timothy's office with a folder full of papers in his hand, and we thought you might like to know about it. We're standing out front with him right now."

"They belonged to my brother, so technically, they're mine," Mick shouted.

Kathleen couldn't make out what he was saying from so far away. "Don't any of you go anywhere. Stay right where you are."

"I can't promise that. Mick was trying to leave when we got here," I said.

"Tell him if he does, he's going to jail. I'll come up with a reason to lock him up later, but I doubt it will be too hard to find."

Kathleen hung up before Annie or I could respond to the threat. As my twin sister put her phone away, I said, "You heard the sheriff. None of us are going anywhere."

"My leg's cramping," Mick complained as he knelt down and rubbed it with his free hand. "I need to go inside and sit down."

I wasn't sure that was such a good idea, but Annie beat me with her own response. "Go on in, then. You can sit down, but we're waiting for the sheriff inside."

Mick appeared to consider running despite his claim to have a cramp, but Kathleen's tone of voice hadn't had an ounce of nonsense in it, and he knew it. "Fine. I still think this is all crazy."

"Indulge us," Annie said as we followed him back into Timothy's office.

Mick stumbled at the entry door and steadied himself by grabbing the doorknob on his way in. Had he really lost his footing, or was he making sure that his fingerprints were added into the mix if Kathleen dusted for prints later? If, as he'd claimed, the front door was already open and the lights had been on when he'd arrived, he would have had no excuse to touch the door earlier. Was it all perfectly innocent, or was Mick lying to us? I had no idea, but I was dying to find out what was so important in that folder.

I didn't get a chance to find out, though, at least not right away. Kathleen showed up before I could get Mick to say a word about it.

"What are you all doing inside?" she asked us, the irritation thick in her voice. "I told you to stay right where you were."

"He had a leg cramp," Annie apologized.

Kathleen looked as though she wanted to comment, but then she decided against it. Turning to Mick, she asked, "How did you get in here?"

"Your siblings walked in with me," Mick said.

"I'm talking about the first time, before they got on the scene." It was clear Kathleen didn't appreciate his sarcasm.

"Like I told them, I came by and found the door open and the lights on. Don't blame me if his assistant left the place wide open."

I spoke up. "We just left Robin. She claimed that she saw someone creeping around the office outside just before she left."

"Well, it wasn't me," Mick said.

Kathleen stared at him a moment, and then she ordered, "Stand up."

"I told you, my leg is cramping."

"I don't really care at the moment. Do as I say." She was using her sheriff's voice, one that commanded instant obedience.

Mick did as he was told, and she knelt down and studied his shoes. "You picked up some mulch on them. Did you realize that?"

Mick shrugged. "After I saw the place was open, I walked around the perimeter to make sure whoever had been in there was gone."

"You've got a story for everything, don't you?" she asked him gravely.

"No stories; just the truth. Now can I sit back down?"

"Fine," she said.

I had to hand it to my sister. I hadn't even considered checking the man's shoes for dirt or mulch. If he'd been the one creeping around the office, of course his shoes would have picked up something from outside. It made me aware yet again that Kathleen was good at what she did. "So, you claim when you arrived that the place was open, so you just walked inside after making sure no one was here. Why were you here in the first place? You have no right to be here."

"As difficult as it is to think about at the moment, I have to consider my future. With Timothy gone, our father's estate is in limbo. For that matter, so is his. I'm his only living relative, which means that this will all be mine anyway, so how could I *not* have the right to be here?"

"Do you have a will to that effect in that folder?" Kathleen asked.

"I'm not sure yet."

"Hand it over and let me see for myself," she commanded, and after a moment's pause, Mick did as she asked.

Kathleen looked through the papers, and then she frowned at Mick. "All I can find here is your father's will. Where is Timothy's?"

"I couldn't find it," he grumbled. "I know state law, though. If he died without one, then I get it all."

"I'm not ready to concede that he didn't have a will of his own," Kathleen said. She turned to Annie and me and asked, "Do you have Robin's phone number?"

Annie nodded.

"Call her and ask her about Timothy's will. If anyone would know about it, it would be her."

I heard Annie have a brief conversation with Robin, and after she hung up, she said, "Robin said it was in the lower locked file cabinet drawer in the closet."

"There's a cabinet in the closet?" Mick asked, clearly peeved that he'd missed it before.

"Apparently," Kathleen said as she got up and moved to the closet behind Timothy's desk. "Did she happen to say where the key was?"

"It's in the top part that's unlocked, filed under the Ks for key," Annie told her.

Kathleen shook her head as she retrieved it. "Cute." After the lower cabinet drawer was unlocked, she made quick work of digging out Timothy's will.

"What does it say?" Mick asked eagerly. "He left it all to me, didn't he?"

"Hold your horses," Kathleen said as she leafed through the document.

"He was my brother. I have a right to know!" Mick demanded.

"Settle down," Kathleen said. "I'm looking."

"You've got a lot of nerve," Annie said to him fiercely. "Timothy couldn't stand you, with good reason, from what I've heard."

"What, did your boyfriend whine to you about his older brother picking on him when he was a kid?" Mick asked sarcastically. "That's what older brothers do."

"Even with the matches and lighter fluid?" she asked him shrilly. "Is that normal in your mind as well?"

Mick shook his head. "Timmy overreacted. He always did that. It wasn't as bad as he probably made it sound."

"I find that hard to believe," I said coldly.

"Great. Now it's three against one. I'm not going to dignify your comments with a response, since you've already tried me and found me guilty. Why let the facts get in the way of a good story?"

"So, you're denying that you tormented him when you were kids?" Annie asked.

"Maybe we didn't get along, but we were still family," Mick said. "Besides, all of that happened when we were kids. We were both grown men, and we put our differences behind us when our father died. You do that when there's no one left in your family but the two of you. Sure, I made some mistakes when we were younger, but I apologized for them, and we got beyond it."

"It's awfully convenient that Timothy isn't around to corroborate that, isn't it?" I asked him.

Mick shrugged. "I don't see how it's any of your business, anyway. I should ask, what were you two doing here? You didn't have any more right to be here than I was. Less, if you ask me."

"We were doing a favor for a friend," Annie said.

"Sure. I bet you were."

"Would you three please pipe down for one minute?" Kathleen asked us.

We all grew quiet as she continued to flip through the will. After a few more moments, she said, "I'm no lawyer, but according to this, Timothy left everything he owned to one person."

"I knew it!" Mick crowed. "He was looking out for his older brother in the end after all."

"You're not the person who gets it all," Kathleen said drily.

"Is it Jenna?" I asked. "Or Robin?"

Kathleen frowned for a second, and then she stared straight at my twin sister. "As a matter of fact, Timothy left it all to you, Annie."

CHAPTER 12: ANNIE

"**M**E?" I ASKED INCREDULOUSLY. "YOU'VE got to be kidding." I'd been close to Timothy once upon a time, but things had been over between us months ago. "Why would he leave everything to me after we broke up?"

"That's what I want to know," Mick said as he reached for the document. "Let me see that!"

He tried to jerk the will from Kathleen's hands, but he'd grossly underestimated her strength, or her determination to keep control of the document. "Sit down, Mr. Roberts."

Mick frowned at us all before doing as he'd been told. "I don't believe it."

"Do you think I'd make something like that up?" Kathleen asked him. She turned to the main page in question and showed it to him. Mick read it with dismay, and then he slumped back in his seat. "Satisfied now?" she asked him.

"Not even a little bit," Mick replied, and then he stared hard at me. "What kind of spell did you weave on my little brother, anyway?"

"We were close, but believe me, I'm just as surprised to hear about this as you are."

"I think I know what might have happened," Pat chimed in.

"Well, I'd love it if you could explain it to the rest of us," I said.

"When you two were dating, you were extremely close. It doesn't surprise me that Timothy named you in his will."

"But he broke up with me," I protested. "Why didn't he change his beneficiary to Jenna?"

"Or me?" Mick added.

I decided to ignore him. "He might have forgotten about it, or he may have left you as his sole beneficiary intentionally. What if he felt so bad about breaking up with you that he didn't have the heart to change his will until he was certain that he and Jenna would last? Maybe he had hopes that someday the two of you would get back together."

Was that possible? Could Pat be right? I had thought at the time we'd been dating that Timothy might have been the one person I could spend the rest of my life with. Had he felt the same way? *Could* we have gotten back together at a later time? I didn't know, and now I never would. If we'd had that chance in our future, someone had robbed us both of it. "I just don't know."

"It's not going to stand up in court," Mick said defiantly. "I'm going to contest it with every penny I have to my name."

"I was under the impression that you were on the verge of bankruptcy," Kathleen said quietly. "How are you going to finance this legal challenge of yours?"

"Have you been investigating me?" Mick asked her.

"Of course I've been investigating you," she said. "Your brother died under mysterious circumstances, you two had a long history of conflict, and you happened to be in town at the time it happened. Did you think there was one chance in ten thousand that I *wouldn't* consider you a suspect?"

"I didn't kill my brother," Mick said.

"So you say," I said.

"I don't want to hear another word out of you, lady," Mick said as he pointed at me.

"As much fun as this has been," Kathleen said, "I think it's time we break up this party, don't you?"

"Fine by me," Mick said as he stood. "I assume that I'm free to go."

"For now, but I wouldn't leave town if I were you," my older sister told him.

"Believe me, I'm not going anywhere until this mess is straightened out." He stared at her for a few seconds, and then he reached out his hand. "Just give me my dad's will back, and then I'll go."

"Sorry, but for the moment, I'm hanging onto it myself."

"It doesn't have anything to do with my brother's death," Mick protested. "You don't have any right to keep it from me."

Kathleen wasn't impressed by his outburst. "That's yet to be determined."

"At least let me have a copy of it," he pled. "Timothy wouldn't show it to me."

Kathleen mulled that over, and then she looked at me. "Annie, there's a copier by Robin's desk. Would you mind?"

"I'd be happy to," I said, taking the document from her and walking into the outer office.

While I was waiting for it to warm up, Pat came out and joined me. "You're going to make a copy for us too, right?"

"Oh, yes. I wonder if Kathleen will let me make one of Timothy's will as well?"

"Seeing as you're the only named beneficiary, I think it's a fair request."

As I made the copies, one set for Mick and another for us, I said, "I still don't get it. Could you be right about Timothy hoping that we'd get together again someday?"

"There's another possibility that I didn't mention earlier," Pat said with a frown.

"Because you didn't want to hurt my feelings, or because you just thought of it?" I asked him.

"A little of both, maybe. What if the version of Timothy's will Kathleen has isn't the latest one? Could this have been an older one that Timothy hadn't gotten around to destroying yet?"

"I don't know. How can we find something like that out?"

"There's only one way I can think of. We need to ask Robin," he said.

"You're right. If anyone would know, she would be the one."

"Let's ask her as soon as we leave here," Pat suggested.

The copies were finished, and I handed Pat one set as I collected the other, as well as the original documents themselves. "Put those in your back pocket, okay?"

"Will do," he said with a grin.

Back in Timothy's office, we found Kathleen and Mick standing there in silence. From the look of things, we hadn't missed anything in our brief absence.

"Here you go," I said as I handed the one visible copy and the original back to my sister.

"Thanks." She handed the copy to Mick, who took it and leafed through the pages before saying a word.

"Is this everything?" he asked me.

"Check the page numbers," I said, insulted that he would imply that I'd shorted him.

He did as I suggested, and thirty seconds later, he nodded. "Okay, I'm satisfied. I still think I should get a copy of Timothy's will, too. After all, I was his brother."

"I need to think about that, but you're free to ask me about it again tomorrow."

"Fine," he said and stormed out of the office, though he managed to glare at me once before exiting.

Kathleen let out a long breath. "Not for nothing, but I don't like that man."

"Don't worry. The more you get to know him, the less he grows on you," I said.

Kathleen held out her hand.

"What?" I asked her as innocently as I could manage.

"Let me have the copy you made for yourself." How could she have possibly known that Pat and I would want our own copy of the document?

"I don't have one," I said, which was strictly the truth, since I'd handed mine over to my brother earlier.

Kathleen didn't even blink as she pivoted and faced Pat. "Then you've got it. There's no way in the world that I'm ever going to believe that you didn't make two copies while you were out there."

Pat didn't even flinch. He just reached into his back pocket and pulled out the folded document. "I'm happy to turn this over, but what can it hurt if we have one, too?" he asked her softly, not even apologizing for not asking her permission first.

Kathleen tapped the paper in her hand, and then she shrugged. "You're right. It can't." She handed the will back to Pat and said, "Who knows? It might even do you some good."

"I know I'm probably pushing my luck, but I really would like a copy of Timothy's will as well," I said. "Kathleen, if he left everything to me, don't I have that right?"

"I don't know about the right, but I'm not going to refuse your request," she said. Before she handed the will over, she said, "Just make one copy of it, okay?"

"We could always make another copy later," Pat said with a grin.

"Once you two delinquents are out of my sight, I don't care what you do."

"Really?" I asked her happily.

"Strike that. Just make the copy."

I made the duplicate, just one, and quickly returned the original to Kathleen. Once I gave it to her, I asked, "Are we leaving now, or can we have a look around?"

"I'm sorry, but I can't allow that," Kathleen said.

"I thought your team had already been through the place?" Pat asked.

"Sure, we looked for the obvious, but it would have been impossible for us to search every piece of paper in this office. I thought we were supposed to be in the modern age of a paperless society. Evidently Timothy didn't believe in that at all."

"He stored stuff on zip drives and on the cloud," I said, remembering Timothy's lecture on the subject once, "but he also believed in having physical backups too, just in case."

"In case of what?" Pat asked me.

"World electronic collapse, I suppose," I said. Something just occurred to me. "Sis, we need a key to lock this place up. You don't happen to have one on you, do you?"

"No," Kathleen said glumly. "It appears that I'll be sticking around after all. Do me a favor and call Robin back. She needs to come down here and lock the place up."

"Again," I said.

"Or for the first time today," Kathleen replied. "I couldn't blame her if she forgot to turn off the lights and lock up after losing her boss early this morning." Our older sister shook her head. "Has it really just been nineteen hours? I'm not sure this day will ever end."

I felt real sympathy for her. "Why don't you go home and get some sleep? Pat and I will hang around and wait for Robin."

"I really shouldn't," she said, though it was clear that was exactly what she wanted and needed to do.

"We won't cross any lines," I promised. "Right, Pat?"

"You have our word," my brother said.

"But you're going to snoop around a little the second I leave though, aren't you?"

I bit my lower lip before responding. "If it's that important to you, we'll sit quietly in Robin's office and wait for her there. We promise."

"That's right. You can trust us," Pat echoed.

Kathleen grinned. "Forget it. I know it would drive you both crazy to do it, so I would never ask you to. Fine. Look around. Just try to put everything back where you found it, okay?"

"Okay," I said.

"Well, go ahead and call her. I'm not going anywhere until I know Robin is on her way."

I did as I was asked, and Robin agreed to come there immediately. If she was afraid that someone was still following her, or even lurking outside her house, she didn't show it.

"She's leaving the house right now," I said after I hung up.

"Then you have six or seven minutes to snoop around to your hearts' content," Kathleen said, grabbing the folder Mick had tried to carry out. "I'll see you two in the morning. Thanks for calling."

"Always," Pat said.

Kathleen just laughed, knowing that we didn't *always* do *anything*, and she drove away.

"Well, what are we waiting for?" Pat asked me as soon as Kathleen's headlights disappeared. "Let's start hunting for something that might be able to help us. Any ideas about where we should start digging?"

"I don't know about you, but I'm dying to see what else was in that locked filing cabinet drawer."

"Let's start there, then."

CHAPTER 13: PAT

"**W**OW, I HAD NO IDEA Timothy did anything like this," Annie said as she pulled the first folder out of the filing cabinet. As she started leafing through it, I leaned over and tried to get a look at what she was talking about.

"What is that?" I asked as I spied a page of handwritten notes.

"Here. See for yourself," she said as she handed it to me.

Timothy had been taking notes about something on the computer. As I scanned the text, I began to feel an unearthly chill.

"Mick wants more than his share, but he's not entitled to any of it. Dad's will says that if Mick challenges me on anything, if he hires an outside attorney, or if he tries to bully me in any way, I'm supposed to cut him off completely. Well, he managed to do all three things at once. Use the attached letter from his attorney to show proof that he doesn't deserve a dime of Dad's money."

"Annie, is there a letter anywhere in that file from Mick's lawyer to Timothy?" I asked my sister.

She looked through the file in question and came up with something. "Do you mean this?"

"I hope so," I said as I took it from her.

Wow. Timothy had been right. As I read the inflammatory letter, I realized that it was all the proof Timothy had needed to cancel his brother's portion of their inheritance. Clearly Mick hadn't liked the fact that Timothy wouldn't give him more than his share, so he'd hired a lawyer to try to bully him into forking over more than he was due. I had a feeling that Timothy's father had known that his elder son would try something, and he'd planned accordingly. That letter was dynamite as far as Mick was concerned. Was that motive enough for murder, though? It most certainly was. If Mick killed Timothy and managed to get that letter back, no one would know that he'd broken the conditions of his father's will. People had been killed for less. "This is what Mick was really looking for," I said as I explained it to Annie and let her read the letter for herself. "Now, all we need to do is check the father's will to make sure it says what Timothy thought it said."

"I've got it right here," Annie said. She scanned the document, and then she suddenly said, "Here it is. *In the event that either son engages an outside attorney to challenge any portion of my last will and testament, or acts in a belligerent or bullying manner in the opinion of the executor, that party will lose any and all rights, bequests, and inheritance from the estate.* Pat, is that legal?"

"I'm not sure about the wording, but the intent is clear, isn't it? I'm not sure how 'belligerent' or 'bullying' are defined, but the letter from Mick's attorney to Timothy seems to qualify, wouldn't you say?"

"I would. So Mick figured if he could find this letter and burn it, he'd get everything."

"He wasn't counting on Timothy being smarter than he was, though," I said. "Hand me that will."

She did as I asked, and after another few moments, I read aloud, "*If one of the beneficiaries should die before the will is probated, the other will receive the full portion of the estate, with the exception of any violation of the challenge provision. If that occurs, any and all moneys will go to the heirs of the beneficiary who did not violate the agreement, and the violating beneficiary will still receive nothing from the estate.* He wanted to make sure that one of his sons didn't kill the other to get all of the inheritance. It sounds kind of gruesome, doesn't it? How much are we talking about here, Annie? This thing implies that there's a great deal of money at stake."

"Hang on. I saw something in his notes about that," Annie said as she checked the folder. "Here it is. Apparently, their father left an estate, after all of the bills had been paid, of a little over two hundred and fifty thousand dollars. That's surely enough for some people to kill for."

"I can't imagine it, but I know that you're right. We need to show this to Kathleen," I said.

"I agree, but let's keep looking before we call her back. There's no telling what else we're going to find. This is better than a diary."

"Okay," I said as I set the handwritten paper, the attorney's letter, and the will aside in a neat little pile. "What else do you have there?"

"This is kind of sweet, actually," Annie said as she showed me a typed note. It said, *"Robin, just wanted to let you know how much I appreciate all that you do for me. It's great having someone as special as you in my corner. Someday you'll learn just how appreciative I am, but in the meantime, know that I couldn't do what I do without you. Timothy."* Below that, written in pen, was a reply. *"Thanks, Boss. You are the best, and it's a real pleasure working with you. Robin."*

"He kept the note," I said. "I didn't realize he was that big a fan of his assistant."

"Timothy had a soft side, too," she said a little wistfully. "I'm going to give this to Robin. I bet she'd appreciate it."

"You should, but let's keep it for now," I answered. "Kathleen might like to see it as well."

"Okay, but remind me to give it to her once this mess is all over," Annie said. After a few moments, she spoke again. "Well, well, well. Would you look at this?"

I tried, but I had trouble reading upside down. "What does it say?"

"It's a set of typewritten notes about some of his clients," she explained. "It's dated a few days before he died."

"That's a lucky break for us. Does he mention anything about Viv or Gordon?"

"As a matter of fact, he does," she said, and then she began to read. *"I need to drop Viv Masters as a client. She's getting tougher to deal with, and I've been forced to be pretty abrupt when rejecting her advances. I'm going to try to end her delusions once and for all. If she continues to pursue me, I don't have much choice. I believe she's unbalanced, and truthfully, I'm a little afraid of her when she shows her temper.* Okay, that's not good for Viv, is it?"

"No. What does he say about Gordon?"

"Gordon Freeman is up to something, and I'm not going to be a part of it. If he wants to do anything illegal, he's going to have to do it without my help. I won't be a party to whatever it is he's up to. I'm dropping him tomorrow. He's not going to like it, and I know that I'm going to have an argument with him that could get dangerous, but I can't risk going to jail. Pat, I had no idea the stress Timothy had been under. Who would have dreamed that being an accountant was such a dangerous occupation?"

"When it comes to money, people do the craziest things. That's why I'm glad we never had much," I said.

"Or ever will," Annie answered with a grin.

"You can't say that anymore, sis, not with Timothy's will leaving everything to you. After what we found in his dad's will, it appears that you're going to get everything from both estates. You're going to be rich."

"I don't want to be, at least not that way," she said.

"If that's the case, you could always just give it away to charity if you're that uncomfortable about it," I told her.

"Let's not do anything premature," she answered with a shrug.

"Fine, but I hope that no matter how much you're worth, you keep working with me at the Iron."

Annie patted my cheek lightly. "Pat, there's nowhere else I'd rather be, and having a little money isn't going to change that."

"I hope not."

We dug through more files, and I was about to wrap it up and move on to something else when I heard someone pull up in front. "Hide those," I told Annie as I closed the file drawer, locked it again, and returned the key to where we'd found it. Annie did as I asked without needing further instruction, shoving the papers we'd found back into the folder along with what we'd held out earlier. She looked around for somewhere to stash them and quickly settled on a large manila envelope that had been used for several different documents over time.

Robin came in a minute later, and I glanced around quickly to be sure we hadn't left anything out in the open. It looked good to me, but I had a feeling that Timothy's assistant would have a better idea than I did if something might be out of place. "I don't know what I must have been thinking," she said as she hung her coat up in a closet. How long was she going to be there? It took her a minute when her coat slid off the hanger and she had to retrieve it, nudging a few file boxes as she did. "We use this mostly for storage, but I like things neat, so it's a good place for my coat. I'm so sorry. I could have sworn that I locked the place up tight when I left, but I was so distraught, it's possible that I forgot."

"Does anyone else have a key?" I asked her.

"No, there were only two. I have one on my ring, and Timothy had one on his."

Annie asked, "Do we know if they found Timothy's keys?"

"You'd have to ask your sister about that," Robin said. She looked around the office and asked, "Who all was here earlier?"

"We found Mick Roberts leaving the building when we got here," I told her as Annie had a conversation with someone on her phone, most likely our older sister.

"So I was right. He was probably the one I saw lurking in the bushes before. What was he doing here?"

"He was looking for his father's will, at least according to him," I said.

Robin frowned. "I had a feeling Mick was involved in this. I told you that earlier, didn't I?"

Yes, along with half a dozen other accusations. "Why do you think he did it?"

"Like I said before, he's been arguing a lot with Timothy lately, and the other morning, he came by and tried to get me to let him wait in his brother's office until he got in. Mick said he wanted to patch things up, but when I refused to allow it, he stormed off. The thing is, I think he was angrier that I wouldn't leave him alone in Timothy's office than he was about anything else. Did you happen to find the will in the file cabinet?"

"We did," I said, not wanting to give her any more details than that.

"Please tell me that Mick doesn't get everything now. That would have broken Timothy's heart. He would have rather seen the money go to a home for stray cats than see his brother get a single penny of it."

"Did you know anything about their father's will, more specifically about the provisions and conditions of inheritance written in it?" I asked her.

She shook her head. "No, Timothy mostly kept that part of his life private from me. The only reason I knew that he kept his will in that cabinet is because he told me about it one day last week. It was the oddest thing. He said that if anything should happen to him, I should look under the file that was marked Future Plans. Is that where you found his will?"

I remembered seeing that it was a blank folder tab. "No, that wasn't where we found it."

"Maybe you didn't find his latest one, then," she said, frowning. "He was pretty clear that the most recent version was in that file folder."

I was about to suggest that we look for it when Annie got off the phone. "Timothy's key to the office wasn't on his ring." Her voice was grim as she conveyed the information to us, and I wondered how much it had taken to get our sister to divulge the information to her.

"So anyone could have had it," I said.

"No, they couldn't have. Timothy never went anywhere without that key," Robin said. "Whoever killed him must have taken it."

"That makes sense," I said. "Let's check that file."

Annie looked alarmed, maybe because we hadn't made copies and replaced what we'd found before Robin had showed up. "What file is that?"

"Did you see one titled Future Plans when you were in there digging out Timothy's will?"

"No, I must have missed that one," Annie admitted.

"I should have mentioned it when you called earlier," Robin said, clearly flustered by her omission. "I guess I must still be in shock."

"Don't beat yourself up about it," Annie said. "Let's grab it and see what it says."

My twin sister retrieved the key as Robin and I watched, and sure enough, she found the file in question. After Annie pulled it out, she locked the door back up and replaced the key as Robin nodded her head in approval. "Here it is." Annie skipped through the document, and when she finished scanning it, she said, "This one is different from the one we found earlier. It's dated four days ago, so I can't imagine we'll find anything that supersedes this."

"Let me take a wild guess. You're not the beneficiary any more, are you?" I asked her.

"I get his cabin and the land it was on, but that's all," Annie said.

"Who gets the rest of it?" I asked her.

"Robin does," my twin sister said, and then the assistant faltered for the second time in twenty-four hours.

CHAPTER 14: ANNIE

"Pat, GRAB HER BEFORE SHE faints again," I yelled at my brother the second I saw Robin begin to sway. He was quick and slid beside her before she lost her footing. It was perfectly understandable. After all, she'd had quite a few shocks to her system lately.

"I'm okay," she said without ever losing consciousness as Pat helped her sit in Timothy's chair. "I can't believe he'd do something that amazing."

I held the document up and checked out the signature on the last page. After I matched it to the one on the will that had named me sole heir, there was no doubt in my mind. "It's legit. It looks as though you're going to inherit the bulk of his estate, Robin."

"He said he was going to look out for me, but I never imagined that was what he meant. I just assumed he'd leave everything to the historical society. He loved the way they took care of our buildings from the past."

"That's who inherits your share if something should befall you," I said. "Let's make sure that doesn't happen though, okay?"

"I'm all for that," she said. "Why would he leave so much to me?"

"Most likely you were the closest person to him lately," Pat said. "He was fighting with Jenna, he and Annie had stopped dating months ago, and we all know what kind of brother he had. Why wouldn't he leave it to you?" I glanced at Annie. "Sorry about that."

"There's nothing to be sorry about," I said. I hadn't even gotten all that excited about the prospect of inheriting it all. After all, it meant that Timothy had to die for it to happen, and I refused to celebrate that. It did touch me that he'd thought enough of me to leave me his cabin and his land, even after our breakup. The cabin was gone, but I promised myself to be a good steward of the land he'd left me. Since it abutted my own property, I would put it to good use by doing absolutely nothing to it, letting the woods and the wildlife reclaim it slowly. It was the most fitting tribute I could think of to honor Timothy's memory.

That, and finding his killer and bringing them to justice.

———— ◦◇◦ ————

"I'm not sure what I should do now," Robin said, clearly baffled by the recent turn of events.

"You need to go home and get some rest," Pat said.

"I'm not at all sure I'm able to drive at this point," she said.

I handed my brother my car keys. "You won't have to. Pat will follow us in my car, and I'll drive you home. How does that sound?"

I saw that Pat was about to protest that he should be the one who drove her when Robin spoke up. "That would be great. Thank you, both of you."

"It's settled, then," I said. As I handed Pat my keys, I looked down at the folder we needed to take with us, which now included the latest version of Timothy's will. "Don't forget to turn out the lights," I said as I tapped it twice.

"I'll take care of it," he said as he put my keys down on the folder in question, making sure that I knew that he'd gotten my message. "I'll see you two there."

Robin started for the door, and then she hesitated. "Let me get my coat first."

"I can do it for you," I said.

"No, I'll do it," she insisted and rushed past me, nearly knocking me aside as she reached for it. "Sorry, but the boxes in there are stacked in a precarious manner, and I would hate for them to tip over on you. Are we ready to go?"

"I'm right behind you," Pat said as he gestured for me to lead Robin out so he could collect the latest evidence we'd just uncovered.

"Come on, then. Let's go," I told Robin as I took her arm. We walked out into the chilly darkness as she handed me her keys.

"Are you sure you don't mind doing this?" she asked me as I let Pat out and then locked the door behind us. No one would be getting in now without a key unless they broke the door down.

"We've got nothing but time," I said, though that wasn't anything near the truth.

As I drove her home, I noticed Robin kept staring behind us. "Annie, someone's following us."

"That would be my brother, remember?" I reminded her gently.

"Oh, yes. Of course. I guess I'm just a little jumpy."

"No worries. You have every right to be," I said as soothingly as I could. "You've been through quite a lot lately."

"Poor, poor Timothy," Robin said as she began to softly weep beside me.

I considered pulling over to comfort her, but then I realized that the best thing I could do for her was to get her safely back home. Once she was there, she could continue to mourn her former boss and benefactor in solitude if that was what she wanted.

As I parked in her driveway, I asked her, "Would you like us to come in for a minute?"

Robin frowned for a second before she spoke. "I know I'm probably being ridiculous, but I'd sleep a lot better if you both went through the place one more time, just to make sure that no one is there."

Pat and I were getting to be her regular security team, but I couldn't begrudge her request. After he joined us, the three of us went inside and made quick work of the inspection. As far as I could tell, nothing had changed since the last time we'd been there so recently.

"Thanks again," Robin said as she saw us out.

"Hang on a second," I said, remembering something.

"What's wrong?" She looked quite alarmed by my request.

"You might need these," I said as I handed her keys to her. I'd held on to them out of habit after unlocking the front door for her, and she took them from me gratefully. "Thanks again."

"You're very welcome. Don't forget to call Kathleen if you get scared tonight." I'd been about to tell her to call me, but I didn't want to be up all night. After all, I'd had a long day myself.

"I will," she said, and again we heard the deadbolt fasten behind us the moment the door closed.

"That was pretty slick," Pat said as he handed my keys back to me.

"What are you talking about?"

"You got to talk to Robin on the drive over," he said. "Did you find anything out that we didn't know before?"

"No. Actually, she was kind of weepy," I said. "Pat, I wasn't trying to outflank you. I just thought she might feel a little more at ease being with another woman."

"You're probably right," my brother said as he nodded in agreement. "That was considerate of you, especially after just losing a fortune to her."

"How could I have lost it? It was never mine in the first place," I said. "I still can't believe he left me the land."

"I know. Timothy had his flaws, but don't we all? In the end, he was a stand-up guy."

"Did you notice one conspicuous absence in the last will?" I asked him.

"You don't mean Mick, do you?"

"No, I doubt Timothy would have left his older brother a bucket of water if he'd been on fire. I'm talking about Jenna."

Pat shook his head. "Annie, they had a completely different relationship than the two of you did. You were friends with Timothy long before you two ever dated. He and Jenna were more of a flash in the pan."

"A flash he'd once considered the love of his life," I reminded him.

"I wonder," Pat said softly as I drove us back to the Iron.

"About what?"

"Could Jenna have believed that she was his beneficiary, since they were dating? It's possible, isn't it?"

"Pat, I know you aren't all that happy with your ex-girlfriend, but she's got a thriving business as a vet. She doesn't need money, certainly not enough to kill for."

"But how do we know that for sure?" Pat asked me. "How do we know that her business is all that successful? For all we know, she could be up to her eyebrows in debt. Killing Timothy may have seemed like the only way out, especially if she suspected she'd inherit his money if he died."

"Wow, that's kind of dark, even for you. Do you honestly think that little of her, Pat? I thought you loved her, at least once upon a time."

"I'm not sure I even know what love is anymore," my brother said sadly. I knew that he'd been devastated when he'd lost Molly, and having Jenna break up with him hadn't made things any easier, but I still had hope that one day he'd find his true love, whether it was Molly or someone else, and what was more, I held the same hope out for myself and our older sister.

"Are you really that cynical these days?" I asked him as we pulled up in front of the Iron.

"I don't know. Maybe. No. Probably not. It's just been a long day, hasn't it?"

"And unfortunately, it's not over yet," I told him.

"What do you mean, Annie? I figured you were dropping me off so I could go to bed and you could head back to your cabin, unless you want to stay with me here again."

"As much as I appreciate the offer, there's no bed like mine, and no home like the one I have. It's just that I'm not going to be there for a while. We need to call Kathleen and show her everything we found this evening. It was our deal, and I'm sticking to it."

"You're right," Pat said with a sigh. "I can't believe this, but I'm getting hungry again. Is there any chance you could whip something up for us while we're waiting on Kathleen?"

"I don't see why not," I said. "It can't be anything all that complicated, though. What did you have in mind?"

He smiled at me, a sight I was happy to see after his temporary depression about being alone. "It's pumpkin season, isn't it? How about some waffles?"

I had to laugh. "Don't you ever get tired of them?"

"The ones you make? Not a chance."

"Okay. I'm on it. I'll get started, and you can call our big sister."

"Why do I have the sudden feeling that you're getting the better part of the deal?" he asked me.

"Maybe because the worst thing that can happen to me is that I can get burned by a waffle iron. That's a lot better than what might happen to you. Make the call."

"Yes, ma'am," Pat said.

As he spoke with our older sister, I started gathering the ingredients I needed for pumpkin waffles. Fortunately I had everything on hand, since I'd been making them since early September. Getting out three of my antique waffle irons, two Wagners and one that didn't have a name that I'd ever been able to find, I set them up as I turned on the gas burners on my stovetop. By the time they all heated up, I'd be ready to start cranking out the delightful treats. I decided to make a quarter of my normal recipe for the three of us; it would leave us with plenty of leftovers unless we were all hungrier than I could imagine, and I figured I could get around twelve large waffles out of the mix. That would be plenty, since they were more filling than standard fare with the added eggs and oats. On the counter, I laid out the waffle mix I used as a base, canned pumpkin, cinnamon, nutmeg, instant oats, vanilla, oil, and eggs. After incorporating them all together, I waited two minutes for the ingredients to rest, and then I was ready to get started making waffles. Some people might have considered it cheating that I used a

101

ready-made mix as my base, but I figured with all of the enhancements I added, it was unique in and of itself. After that, it was simply a matter of adding batter to the irons after spraying them with some nonstick spray, adding a little over half a cup of batter to each iron, and then waiting two minutes before I turned them to give the other side a minute and a half to finish off. My irons didn't produce as consistently uniform waffles as a modern iron would have, but I enjoyed using the old ways whenever I could, and this was certainly one of those times.

"She's on her way," Pat said as he grabbed one of the first hot waffles ready after setting three places—plates, silverware, and glasses—and adding butter and syrup to the counter as well.

"We need to get someone in to look at the big fridge unit," I told Pat as I kept producing more waffles. "It's on the fritz again."

"I can call someone tomorrow," my brother said, talking with his mouth nearly full of waffle.

"That might be too late. Somebody needs to check on it during the night to make sure it's still working."

"I have a hunch who that someone will be," Pat said with a shrug. "What can I do if it stops?"

"Jiggle this"—I showed him—"and give it a good rap right here." I demonstrated.

"And that fixes it?" he asked incredulously.

"No, but it usually starts working again after I do that," I answered with a smile. "Promise me you'll check on it tonight."

"I promise," he said. "I should at least get another waffle for getting up in the middle of the night."

"Fine by me. Here you go," I said as I put a fresh one on his plate.

<hr />

Kathleen came in frowning, but she smiled as soon as she got a whiff of the air. "Pumpkin pancakes. My favorite."

"Actually, they are waffles," I said with a smile of my own.

"Let me restate that. Pancake waffles. My favorite."

"You were late, so we waited," Pat said with a grin, and then he jammed a large section of waffle into his mouth, letting a little butter and syrup run down his chin in the process.

"You always were a true gentleman," Kathleen said as she took a seat at the counter beside our brother. "I'll wait for you, Annie, even if he won't."

"You have my blessing to go ahead," I said as I put a hot waffle on her plate. "They're better when they're hot."

"I think they're good all of the time," Pat said as he tried to commandeer Kathleen's waffle.

She was too fast for him, though. Her fork blocked his perfectly, and Pat shrugged and gave up. "There's always the next batch."

"Yes, there is," Kathleen said as she doctored her waffle and took a large bite. "This is amazing. My compliments to the chef."

"The chef thanks you," I said with a grin, happy to have my immediate family together, no matter the circumstances. "Should we tell you what we found now or wait until after we've eaten?"

"Let's wait," Kathleen said. "I'd like to enjoy these as long as they last."

"Agreed," I said as I reloaded the three irons. By the time I was out of batter, we'd all eaten our fill of waffles, and we still had four large waffles left over. Frankly, I'd been amazed by how much we'd managed to eat between the three of us.

As I started to clean up, Pat and Kathleen moved the dishes over into the sink and wiped the counter down.

After Pat dried it, he asked, "Do we still have to wait for Annie to finish?"

"I can add to the conversation just fine from over here," I said. "Go ahead and spread things out on the countertop so we can bring Kathleen up to date on what we found."

"I appreciate the food, and the call," our sister said as she stifled a yawn.

"Do you want to catch a quick nap upstairs before we get started?"

Pat asked her. "I have a perfectly good couch up there, or you could even take the bed, if you'd like."

"I appreciate the offer, but if I lie down for two minutes, I won't wake up until morning. Let's go ahead and get started."

"As you wish," he said, and then he began to lay things out in piles so our findings would be easier to explain.

CHAPTER 15: PAT

"Wow, you two have been busy," Kathleen said as she surveyed all of our finds. "Where was all of this?"

"We found it all in a file cabinet in Timothy's closet," I said. "We never would have known where to look if we hadn't spoken to Robin. She's been really helpful to us so far."

"Let's go through it step by step," our sister suggested.

Annie reached for the first pile, which happened to include Timothy's father's will and the letter from Mick's attorney. "It turns out that Mick managed to write himself out of his dad's will," she said as she read the clause as well as the letter.

"Do you think he knew about the conditions beforehand?" Kathleen asked us.

"I can't imagine anyone being that stupid," I said.

Annie interjected, "You don't know Mick that well, though. He might have been under the mistaken impression that he could bulldoze Timothy like he did when they were younger. Timothy wouldn't have put up with it as an adult, though."

"So let me get this straight. Is it your belief that Mick realized he wouldn't be able to bully his brother with a letter from an attorney, and he knew that he'd made a huge mistake trying? That would mean that his only option was to kill his brother and then break into his office, steal the will and the letter, and then file it with the state so he could collect both shares of the inheritance."

"It's one scenario we're considering," I said.

"But just one," Annie added. "Look at this."

She handed Kathleen the typed sheet we'd found in the folder accusing Viv of being unbalanced, delusional, and in possession of a demonic temper. I also pointed out the section that claimed Gordon was doing something illegal that Timothy wouldn't be a part of and that he was afraid of the man's volatility as well as his dark connections. "Why would he create a document like this?" Kathleen asked as she tapped the sheet with her finger.

"I'm guessing that he wrote things out to help him plan out his next moves," I suggested. "Did you ever see any evidence of him doing anything like this when you two were together?" I asked Annie.

"No, but that doesn't mean that he didn't do it in his office. Timothy was pretty private about his work. He didn't like to talk about it, and in particular, any discussion about his clientele was strictly off limits."

Kathleen nodded as she moved on to the next group. "What's this?" she asked as she picked up the note that went back and forth from Timothy to Robin.

"That's not really part of the case," Annie said. "We thought Robin might like to have it once we showed it to you. It helps explain why Timothy left her everything." She handed Kathleen the last will we'd found, and the sheriff read it with interest.

"Nearly everything," Kathleen corrected her as she pointed to the document. "It appears that you at least get some land, Annie."

"It was sweet of him to do it. I certainly wasn't expecting it."

"I think it's nice, too," Kathleen said.

"Is there any risk that folks are going to think it gives you a motive to kill Timothy?" I asked her.

"I don't see how. That land isn't worth much without the cabin," Annie protested. "Besides, if I wanted to inherit enough to make it worth my while, would I have burned the cabin down?"

"While it may be true, it's not exactly an argument you can make in public," I said.

"Let people talk if they make up their minds to," Annie answered. "I'm not going to let it bother me one way or the other."

"Good for you," Kathleen said. "If anything, this gives Robin some incentive to do away with her boss. Is there anything that might make you want to take her off of your list?"

"Nothing specific, though the note shows some real affection between the two of them," I said. "How about you, Annie?"

"She stays until we find something else out that clears her."

Kathleen frowned in thought for a moment before asking, "I'm curious about something. Was she surprised by the contents of the new will?"

"She nearly fainted," I said.

"Nearly, but not quite," Annie replied.

"Do *you* think she was faking it?" I asked her.

"I honestly couldn't say. I'm afraid at this point that I'm having trouble trusting my instincts. I don't believe anyone, even Jenna."

"Why not Jenna?" Kathleen asked her.

"When we went by her place to speak with her, she was having a bit of a fire outside," I explained.

"Nothing wrong with that. It was a bit chilly today."

"She wasn't burning wood, though," Annie explained.

"Then what was she burning?"

"Mostly old paperwork," I answered. "She claimed that it was all old business information, but Annie said that she could swear that she saw a card in the flames with Timothy's handwriting on it."

"It's true," my twin sister said. "I'm not sure why she would burn that."

"Maybe she couldn't take any memories of him around anymore," I suggested.

"Or maybe she has a guilty conscience about what she did to him," Kathleen said.

"Do you think she might have actually done it?" I asked her. It didn't match the woman I'd dated, but then again, how well did I really know her?

"Anything's possible. That's all I can say after all of my years on the job. Do you mind if I take all of this with me?"

I suddenly realized that there was something I'd forgotten to do. "Would I be out of line if I asked you if we could make copies of everything for ourselves first?"

Kathleen was about to protest, but after a moment of internal struggle, she shrugged. "Why stop now? I've got to give you credit for at least asking me first this time."

"Don't give us too much," Annie said with a grin as she gathered the papers up. "We didn't have a great deal of time before you got here, and to be honest with you, it kind of slipped our minds."

"Just go do it, and be quick about it," Kathleen said good-naturedly. "If I weren't so full right now, I might protest, but don't push your luck."

"I'll be back in a flash," she said.

Once she was gone, Kathleen said softly, "Annie's doing a little better, isn't she?"

"She's rattled, there's no doubt about it, but I think she's starting to get a handle on things," I said, feeling a bit like a traitor tattling on my twin sister. I knew Kathleen's question had come from a good place, but I still didn't like to tell tales out of school on Annie. "What can I say? She's coping. I asked her to stay here with me again tonight, but she turned me down."

"Yeah, I thought about making the same offer myself, but I know that she wouldn't accept it either, so why bother? Annie loves her cabin in the woods, and I'm not even sure she's not right wanting to be there. After all, it's the one place on earth that's entirely hers."

"Still, it wouldn't hurt to make the offer," I said. "She might like hearing it from you, too."

"Of course," Kathleen said, and then she stared off into space for a few moments before she looked at me again. "Pat, what's your take on this mess?"

I thought about it, and then I realized that it was too soon to say anything just yet. "You know how it goes. You collect pieces until they begin to fit together. Often it's not until the last second that things manage to come together."

Kathleen nodded. "You two have become pretty adept at this, haven't you?"

"We do our best, but we both fully realize that we're no match for you," I said sincerely. It wasn't a matter of buttering our older sister up; it was the complete and unvarnished truth.

"Maybe, but folks open up to the two of you in ways they won't with me. I have the authority of the law behind me, for all the good that it does me sometimes, but you two tap into the community in ways that I never could."

"So then we complement each other," I said.

"You do look nice tonight," Kathleen answered with a grin. It was an old game we'd played a thousand times in our lives, intentionally misunderstanding each other.

"Thank you kindly, ma'am," I said as Annie walked back in, carrying two sets of papers now.

"What are you two talking about?" she asked.

"How good I look tonight," I said with a laugh.

"I don't know about that, but I have a hunch that's not all you were discussing. Were my ears burning for a reason, or was I the topic of conversation?"

She was good; I had to give her that. "We were just discussing the fact that you turned down my offer to stay with me tonight," I said.

"And I'm pretty sure you're going to turn me down, too," Kathleen added. "The offer is good, though. It's not too late to reconsider. You won't hurt our feelings, either way."

"As much as I appreciate the offers, I'm going to have to take a hard pass. I want to go home as soon as we're finished here." She paused to grin at me as she added, "Besides, Pat has to get up in the middle of the night to check on our fridge, and if I hang around here, he'll probably make me do it."

"I wish I could say that you were wrong, but I can't," I replied with the hint of a grin. "Are we finished here, ladies?"

Kathleen stifled a yawn as she stood and took one set of the documents from Annie. "These are the originals, I presume?"

"Yes, ma'am, as original as a copy of a copy can be. Will we see you in the morning?"

"You can count on it," she said as she headed for the door. "Are you coming?"

Annie glanced at me before answering. "I don't know, am I?"

"I don't know about you, but I'm finished for tonight. I need to get to sleep, especially if I'm getting up in a few hours," I said with a grin.

"Then I'll say good night."

After my sisters were gone, I locked up and turned off all of the lights. Before going to bed upstairs, I set my alarm for two a.m. It would be impossible for me to wake up otherwise, and I knew if our fridge conked out before we could get it repaired, we'd lose quite a bit in inventory for the grill.

At two a.m., I nearly hit the snooze button on my alarm clock out of habit, but something made me wake up enough to manage to get out of bed. I didn't turn on any lights since there was a faint glow coming from the light outside the building, giving me enough illumination to see without destroying my night vision. Hopefully I would find the fridge running fine and be back in bed before I had a chance to come fully awake.

It was running like a champ, humming happily away when I checked it, and as I glanced toward the front, I noticed that the quality of the light outside suddenly changed.

Instead of the steady illumination of the lamp, the light was now flickering.

Hurrying to the front, I glanced outside and saw that one of our wooden rocking chairs was on fire!

Grabbing the fire extinguisher, I flipped on the lights—both inside and out—unlocked the door, and put the flames out before they could do much damage to the front porch, let alone the entire building. Once the fire had been extinguished, I pulled the chair off the porch using a towel from Annie's grill and set it in the gravel where it couldn't do any harm if it should happen to spontaneously combust again.

It was clear that someone had tried to burn the Cast Iron Store and Grill to the ground, and by the oddest of flukes, I'd caught it in time before it could do any real damage. Once I was sure everything was fine, I went back inside, got dressed, and then I made two phone calls that I wasn't all that excited about making.

Kathleen showed up first. I was relieved to see that she kept her siren and lights off, but she nearly hit me when she raced into our parking lot. She still wore her uniform, as wrinkled as it was. "What happened?"

"I told you pretty much everything over the phone."

Kathleen checked the chair, smelled it, and then she rubbed her hands over parts of it. After that, she did the same thing with the scorched section of the porch. "That was good work putting it out so quickly," she said. "I smelled traces of gasoline. It could have been really bad."

"Thank our cranky fridge," I said. "That was the only reason I saw it in time." She reached for her radio, but I stopped her. "What are you doing?"

"I'm getting a team out here," she said, looking puzzled by my question.

"What good are they going to do?" I asked. "Why don't we keep this between ourselves?"

"Have you completely lost your mind?" Kathleen asked me. "This isn't a fluke, and you know it. Someone just tried to burn you out, and if you hadn't spotted it in time, they might have succeeded."

"I get that, but think how puzzled the arsonist is going to be when no one is talking about it in the morning. We might be able to use that to our advantage."

"What did you have in mind?" Kathleen asked as she put her radio back into its clip.

"I don't know yet, but what do we gain by calling in reinforcements at this point? You know, Annie knows, and so do I. The only other person who knows is the one who set the fire. Let's keep that to ourselves for the moment."

"We can do that," she said, "although it's against my better judgment. What makes you think they won't try again?"

"I don't, but I'd still like a chance to brace everyone about what happened here first."

Annie drove up, saw the burned chair in the gravel, and then she hugged me. "Pat, are you okay?"

"I'm fine," I replied. "I didn't even get smudged, let alone burned."

"That's not funny, Patrick," she said before turning to Kathleen. "I figured you'd have an entire forensic team here by now."

"Our brother wants to keep the lid on what happened," she explained. After she told Annie my reasons, my twin sister nodded. "I like it. Wow, am I glad that fridge was acting up. I almost don't want to get it fixed now."

"Well, I do," I said. "One early-morning wake-up call is enough for me, and now I've had them two nights in a row. Let's everybody go back to sleep and discuss this in the morning. How does that sound?"

"Good, except I'm staying here again with you, and don't try to talk me out of it," Annie said. "I want to blow up one of the air mattresses and sleep downstairs tonight in case the arsonist comes back."

"Mind if I join you?" I asked, knowing that I'd feel better having her there with me.

"Sure, why not?" Annie turned to Kathleen. "How about you? Care to make it all three of us?"

"If you need me, I'll stay," she said.

"There's really no need, Kathleen. We'll be fine on our own. I just didn't want to leave you out," Annie said.

"No worries, then. I have a hunch that whoever did this wouldn't come within a mile of this place until morning, so you should be safe, and I've slept on those air mattresses before, remember? My back is still hurting from the last time."

"That's because you're getting old and feeble," I told her with a grin.

"I'll race you any day, little brother. Just name the time and place."

"That's never going to happen," I said, holding my smile. "Thanks for rushing over."

"Hey, even if it weren't my job, we're family, right?"

"Right," I said.

After she was gone, Annie and I set up the air mattresses and sleeping bags. I wasn't expecting to fall asleep given the circumstances and what had just happened, but to my surprise and delight, I didn't wake up until sunshine streaming into the Iron hit my face.

I'd somehow managed to fall asleep after all, and from the looks of my sister, she'd managed to nod off as well.

CHAPTER 16: ANNIE

P AT AND I GOT UP in plenty of time to get ready before we opened the Iron for the day. I had some clothes stashed there for emergencies, but I was running out, which was fine with me. No matter what, I'd be sleeping in my own bed tonight.

While he was still asleep, I crept upstairs, took a shower, and changed, and then I returned downstairs to find him awake.

Pat surprised me by sitting up from his air mattress. "How did you sleep?"

"Off and on," I admitted. "How about you?"

"The same. At least our pyromaniac didn't come back." He stood and stretched, and then he began to deflate the mattresses.

"Do you need any help with that?" I offered.

"Thanks, but why don't you get started in the kitchen? I wouldn't mind some bacon and eggs this morning before we open. Is there time?"

I glanced at one of the big clocks we had on display. "We're good. As a matter of fact, I think I'll join you."

As Pat disappeared upstairs, I got busy prepping some bread and the day's specialty, a Tex-Mex meal that simmered in a cast iron pot on top of the grill. I'd also offer my standard fare of burgers and hot dogs as well as hot sandwiches, but I liked to have at least one different choice every day. After the main course was prepped and simmering away, I made some sausage gravy and started frying our turkey bacon. I wasn't sure if Pat knew that I'd been substituting turkey for pork for the past few months, but if he'd noticed, he must not have minded. Not only was it less expensive, but it was healthier for us as well.

When he rejoined me, the bacon was ready, the toast was set to go down into the toaster, and I had seven eggs out. "Scrambled okay?" I asked him.

"If I don't have to make them, they can be hardboiled for all I care," he said. After taking a deep breath, he added, "If that's coffee, I'd love some."

"I'm way ahead of you," I replied as I poured him a cup.

The first round of biscuits were ready to come out of one of my ovens, and as I put the pan on the rack to cool, Pat asked, "Is it too late to change my mind?"

"About the eggs?"

"No, that part still sounds good, but there is no way I'm going to be able to pass up sausage gravy and biscuits."

The sausage was straight pork, enhanced with seasonings. So much for trying to feed him healthier, but I couldn't refuse. In fact, I decided to have the same thing myself, substituting bacon and toast for a hot biscuit, split and buttered, and then smothered in sausage gravy.

It was delicious, but I'd have to start cutting back on what I ate or I was going to have to buy a complete new wardrobe two sizes larger, and that was something I was not at all eager to do.

After we ate, I cleaned up and got ready for our first customers of the day, while Pat consulted with Skip about his plans for finishing our Christmas display. Edith glided in on her own, and after a few greetings, she ensconced herself back in her postal lair.

I was ready for our first customer of the day when Pat unlocked the front door.

At least I thought I was.

But then someone stomped in, putting a damper on what had been, up to that point, a pretty good day.

"What can I do for you, Gordon?" Pat asked one of our suspects as I joined them up front.

"You can call off that she-devil of a sister of yours," Gordon said angrily.

I smiled sweetly at him. "I can't imagine what I might have done to upset you."

"I'm not talking about you," he growled, "and you know it. I mean the sheriff. She needs to stop coming around my business, or there's going to be real trouble."

"Are you threatening Kathleen?" Pat asked angrily, and I was right there with him. We might tease among ourselves, but no one, and I mean no one, threatened one of us without consequences.

To my surprise, Gordon lost quite a bit of his volume as he responded, "I don't mean she's going to be in trouble. I'm talking about me."

That was interesting. "Why? What's going on?" I asked him.

"There are some folks I work with who aren't the most understanding people in the world, if you know what I mean. I never realized they were keeping an eye on my dry-cleaning business until this morning. Your sister wasn't gone three minutes before there was a knock on my door. I was told in no uncertain terms that if I didn't extract myself from this investigation, and fast, I'd be looking for more than a new business to run."

"Did they actually threaten you?" Pat asked him. "You should speak to someone in law enforcement about that."

"What are you trying to do, get me killed?" he asked, his voice going a little higher and louder as he said it.

"No, but you can't just let someone threaten you like that," my brother replied.

"You don't understand. I have no choice." He took a deep breath, and then he said, "I need your sister to hear something."

"Why didn't you tell her earlier?" I asked him. "You said she just left your shop."

"I couldn't talk to her there. I'm pretty sure the place is bugged."

Was this man rampantly paranoid, or was someone really keeping tabs on him? "Your friends, I take it?" Pat asked.

"If you can call them that," Gordon answered.

"Why don't you just call her?" I suggested.

"I will, if I can use your phone."

"Do you honestly think your cell phone is tapped, too?" I asked him. What kind of people was he mixed up with, anyway?

"I don't know, but I'm not willing to take the chance. Will you talk to her for me?"

Pat frowned, and then he shook his head. "No."

"No? Please. I'm begging you."

"I'll call her on my phone, and you can speak with her directly yourself," Pat said firmly. "That's the most I'm willing to do."

I wasn't sure that I would have been able to take the same firm stand my brother just had, but I certainly wasn't going to go contradict him. We always did our best to speak with one voice, particularly when we were investigating a case.

"If that's the best you can do, then I guess I'll just have to take it."

Pat nodded, dialed Kathleen's number, and then he said, "Someone here wants to speak with you." After that, he handed Gordon his phone, and then he moved over next to me so he could hear their conversation, too.

"Listen, you have to stop coming by my shop. I know, but it looks bad. Okay. Sure. I'm going to tell you something now that could get me in a lot of trouble. Why would I do that? Because the people I'm in too deep with could do a lot more than lock me up. I was making a pickup in Charlotte at about the time Timothy was murdered. No, I can't give you the guy's name, but I stopped off at an all-night convenience store to get something for my stomach right before I left, and I know I'm on their security tape. Yes, I saw it in the corner." After he gave her the address, he said, "Okay. I understand that. If there's a problem, find a way to tell me about it without coming by my business, would you? Fine."

He hung up the phone and handed it back to Pat.

"You really are scared of these people, aren't you?" I asked.

Gordon shrugged. "I didn't say what I was picking up. If nobody digs too hard into that angle of it, I should be fine. Well, at least I'll be better off than I am at the moment. Thanks for helping."

"You're welcome," Pat said. "Just out of curiosity, what were you picking up?"

"Paper towels," he said with a grimace. "Boxes and boxes of paper towels."

That might have been what it said on the outside of the boxes he'd collected, but I doubted seriously that was the contents inside. "Okay," Pat said.

Gordon must have smelled the sausage gravy simmering on the stovetop. "That smells great."

"Would you like a bite to eat before you go?" I asked.

Pat looked at me oddly, but hey, I ran the grill, and I hadn't turned anyone away yet, even one of our suspects, though it seemed to me that he'd just cleared himself of suspicion.

"No, I couldn't. Thanks for offering, though."

After he was gone, I asked Pat, "What do you think?"

"I believe the man is honestly in fear for his life."

"Wouldn't that give him reason to lie to us?" I asked.

"Probably, but I'm willing to bet that Kathleen is going to find him on that security surveillance. Why else give her so much potentially damaging evidence?"

"Like he said, it wasn't all that damaging."

"Not unless our sister decides that she doesn't like being messed with," Pat answered. "Until we hear otherwise though, I think we can take Gordon off our list of suspects."

"I'm fine with that," I said as two customers came into the store. One headed for the section of screws in Pat's department, while the other headed straight back to my grill. "Talk to you later," I said, and then I started doing what I was meant to do, feed the hungry people of Maple Crest good food for a fair price.

There were worse callings I could have had, and I knew it.

Though we didn't see any of our other suspects at the Iron for the rest of the day, that didn't mean that it wasn't without its own drama. Two of our senior citizen ladies got into an argument over a birdbath Pat had marked down for quick sale, each woman claiming to have seen it first. Pat, using the skills and wisdom of Solomon, figured out a way to get them to compromise. Harriet got the birdbath, but Jeanie got a feeder she'd had her eye on, for our cost as well. In the end, both women left the shop happy, something that didn't always happen at the Iron.

• ❧ •

By the time we were ready to close up for the day, Pat and I had come up with a solid game plan for our investigation.

We were going to do a little pot stirring and see what bubbled to the top.

After all, we still had a healthy list of suspects to consider, and fortunately, there was a little leverage for us to use on each of them now.

CHAPTER 17: PAT

"**A**RE YOU READY TO ROLL?" I asked Annie as I approached the grill in the back of the store.

"Just about," she said as she put the last pot away. "How about you?"

"I'm ready," I told her. "I sent Skip on with the deposit, so we could get going."

That was interesting. "What, no drop-in visit?"

"For your information, I don't plan my entire schedule around my banking needs."

"What's wrong, Pat, is she off today?"

It was hard to get angry with Annie, especially when she was grinning at me like she was. I found myself laughing right along with her. "Carly's off today, but nothing's going to happen there."

"Why not? Have I been teasing you too much about her lately?"

"Yes," I said as I held the front door open for her. "But that's beside the point. I just found out that she's got a boyfriend in Boone. He's a professor at the college there."

"I'm sorry," Annie said, her smile vanishing. "That's too bad."

"Not really. You know, when it comes right down to it, I believe I had my shot at true love, and I blew it."

"Why do I get the feeling that you're not talking about Jenna?" my twin sister asked me as I locked the door behind us after turning off the lights. I couldn't help but glance over at where the scorch marks were on the porch, though I'd put a rug over the worst of it, and I'd replaced the burnt chair with another.

"What can I say? You always could read me like a book," I said.

"To be fair, it's not like it's applied mathematics," she answered. "It's more like a connect-the-dots book we had as kids. Point A, that's you, connects directly to Point B, that's Molly. It's the simplest puzzle in the world."

"I wish I could say that you were full of hot air," I told her.

"But you can't, so you won't," Annie answered.

I decided that particular line of conversation wasn't getting us anywhere. "Which of our suspects should we tackle first?"

"I think Jenna would be appropriate, don't you?" she asked.

"Why Jenna?" I asked her. "Because this seems to be the afternoon we discuss the ghosts of girlfriends past?"

"No, it's mainly because I'm not entirely satisfied with her story," Annie said. "What if she killed Timothy to hide something he knew about her?"

"What could that possibly be?"

"I don't know. Maybe she's hooked on horse tranquilizers. She's a vet, isn't she?"

"I can't see that happening," I said, unable to keep myself from defending her, even though she'd discarded me pretty thoroughly not that long ago.

"But it's possible," Annie insisted. "Say that's not it, then. How about if she's been defrauding the government somehow, and Timothy found out about it?"

We got into her Subaru and drove as we continued the discussion. The sooner we got to Jenna's practice, the sooner I could get out of this onerous conversation. "I don't think so."

"It might be true, though. That's the point. Pat, she was burning records and personal information when we saw her yesterday. Even you can't deny that."

"What do you mean, even me?" I asked her.

"Come on. Every time I bring something up, you dismiss it out of hand."

I thought about it and realized that she was right. "Okay, I'll admit that last one's possible. It could explain why she felt the need to torch so many pages. If she were covering her tracks, it might make sense to her to burn it all down to ashes. What about the card we saw, though?"

"If Timothy was going to turn her in to the authorities, would she keep a sentimental card she got from him? I know I wouldn't."

"That's because you're tougher than the average bear," I told her. "Let's say for the sake of argument that you're right. How are we going to catch her in a lie?"

"There's only one way I can think of short of hiring a forensic accountant, which Kathleen may have to end up doing eventually. We need to push her until she snaps and tells us something she meant to keep to herself."

"Oh, boy. This is going to be fun, isn't it?"

"If you'd rather skip it, you could always wait in the car," Annie suggested.

I shook my head as I looked at my twin sister. "No thanks."

"Good, because I need you in there with me. We're here," she said as we pulled into Jenna's practice parking lot. It was empty though.

"No one's here," I said, fighting to keep the relief out of my voice.

"Jenna is; at least her truck is," Annie said, pointing to the back of the building. "Maybe we'll luck out and catch her alone."

"Do we ever get that lucky?" I asked her.

"No, but that just means that we're due."

The front door to Jenna's clinic was locked, and I was ready to give up, since I didn't want to be there in the first place. "Nobody's home after all."

Annie swatted at me, and then she pointed to a sign. "*For access after regular hours, ring the bell. If no one answers, call our service and leave a detailed message.*" After a smug little grin, she reached over and rang the bell.

Jenna answered our summons almost immediately. Had she seen us drive up? Was she waiting by the door, hoping that we'd give up and go away? If so, then why did she answer at all?

"We saw your truck in back," Annie said. That answered the questions I'd just raised in my head. How did my twin sister do that?

"I was just heading out," Jenna said, startled to see us. "I thought we were finished yesterday, so unless you have a sick pet, you'll have to excuse me."

There was no way we were going to be able to grill her in detail. I was going to have to take a hard, strong shot at her and hope for a reaction. Otherwise, we wouldn't learn a thing.

"Why did you burn that card from Timothy yesterday?" I asked her point blank.

I even managed to catch Annie by surprise with the ambush. It took Jenna a moment to compose herself before she replied. "Odd. I don't remember that being in the pile."

"We both saw it, so there's no use trying to deny it," I said, refusing to move out of her way. I was being intentionally obnoxious, and I realized at that moment that even if Jenna had pled with me to take her back, I wouldn't have been interested. I was burning the bridge and making sure there was no going back to her when this was all over, assuming that she hadn't been the one to kill Timothy. "Don't lie to us."

Jenna stared at me steadily for a few seconds, and then she said in a cold, dead voice, "Patrick, I don't care about you enough to lie to you. It was nobody's business, and it certainly isn't any of yours. Tell your sister that I want any correspondence she finds at Timothy's that originated with me."

"Did you hear that, or do I need to repeat it to you?" I asked Annie, trying to warm the air a little with a joke, and failing miserably at it.

"I meant Kathleen, and you know it. Now get out of my way. I have work to do."

The look she gave me as she brushed past me would have frozen a lava flow in its tracks.

"Wow, that was painful to watch, even for me," Annie said once Jenna was gone.

"You said we needed to push her," I reminded her.

"Push, not demolish," she said.

"Do you think I went too far?"

"No, the more I think about it, that was the only way to handle her." Annie touched my shoulder lightly. "Pat, are you okay?"

"I'll live," I said as we headed back to her Subaru.

"You know you'll never be able to repair the damage you just did, don't you?" Annie asked me in a soft voice.

"I knew it before I opened my mouth," I told her. "I wonder what she was talking about being at Timothy's office. Could there be something there that might convict her?"

"It's possible. Then again, it could have just been a set of mushy letters she didn't want anyone else to read," Annie countered.

"Now you tell me that. I don't know. Has Jenna ever struck you as the type to get embarrassed by much of anything?"

"I can't really say. After all, you know her better than I do," Annie said.

"Quit ducking and answer the question."

"No," my twin sister said slowly. "There *might* be something to it, but how are we going to get back into Timothy's office to find out? We can't ask Kathleen to let us in again so soon, and we can't exactly borrow the key from Robin."

"I'm not so sure about that," I said as a plan started to hatch in my mind.

"Do you honestly think she'd just hand it over to us?"

"No, but what if we took it and then returned it without her knowing about it?" I asked.

"You mean steal it, don't you? Don't get me wrong; I don't disapprove. I just want to make sure we are talking about the same thing."

"Yes, I mean steal it, if you want to put too fine a point on it."

Annie laughed. "That's about the only point we could use, isn't it? I can't think of anything better to do at the moment, so it sounds like a plan to me. Should we go after it now or wait until after we check in with Viv and then Mick?"

"I'm not in the mood to tackle Mick at the moment, and I'm going to have to figure out a way to get Robin's key to the office without her knowing it, so I guess Viv wins by default."

"The hairdresser's shop it is," Annie said. "I'm proud of you, little brother."

"Why? Is it just in general, or is there a reason in particular?"

"It's about Jenna. You two don't belong together. I'm just glad you're finally seeing it for yourself."

"For all the good it's going to do me. Let's go."

———— ⊷⊶ ————

Viv was in her shop, but she was busy this time, as were her two assistants. No one was waiting though, and she was just finishing up with her customer. "You two are back again?" she asked, clearly unhappy about our presence in her shop again so soon after our last visit.

"We won't take more than a minute," I said.

"Sit over there and wait for me, then," Viv instructed us, and then she turned back to her client. "Like I said, Ruth, that color makes you look ten years younger."

If that were the case, I would have hated to see how old the woman looked upon her arrival. I decided to keep that to myself, though. Annie reached over and plucked a magazine from the nearby table, but there was nothing there I could even feign interest in, so I just sat in silence. Two minutes later, Viv pointed to us and motioned for us to go outside. Her last appointment had exited a minute earlier, and I'd been waiting on her signal.

"Let's go," I told Annie. "We're up."

"After you," my sister said as she put the magazine back where she'd found it.

Viv was standing outside smoking a cigarette when we went out. "I have three minutes before my next appointment. If the smoke bothers you, no one asked you to be here in the first place."

It was rude and abrupt, much like I'd been with Jenna. Apparently I wasn't going to be able to repeat my earlier performance.

I didn't have to. Annie stepped in before I could say a word.

"Blow us off if you want, Viv, but we're here as a courtesy before we go speak with the sheriff."

It was an outstanding bluff, and quite an opening line. I for one was curious about where she was going with it, and I had to wonder if she knew herself.

"What do you think you know?" Viv asked, openly glaring at both of us now.

"Timothy said you were dangerous and unbalanced and that you wouldn't take no for an answer. He was getting ready to fire you as a client. Did you know that?"

Viv looked as though she'd just smelled something rotten. "What does it matter at this point? I don't care anymore."

"Why? Because he's dead?" I asked pointedly.

"No, because he rejected me one too many times, and even if he were still alive, I did something so stupid that he would never be able to forgive me."

"What could you have possibly done that was so bad?" Annie asked her.

"I slept with that jerk brother of his, Mick," she confessed.

"When did this happen?" Annie asked, pushing her for more details.

"The night Timothy was murdered. I met Mick at the bar outside of town, and I let him pick me up. It was my way of showing that snob of a brother of his that I wasn't going to wait around forever for him to come to his senses. The irony of it was that Mick was with me even while Timothy was being murdered. I did it all for nothing. He never knew what I'd done."

"Why didn't you tell anyone this before?" Annie asked her gently. "You lied to us earlier when you said that you'd been home alone."

"Wouldn't you have? What alternative did I have? Could you have admitted taking Mick Roberts home?" she asked Annie pointedly.

"No, not unless it was under gunpoint," Annie admitted. "So, why tell us now?"

"I knew that if I didn't, you two would keep hounding me until I told you the truth. Besides, like I said, what does it matter now? It's over. All of it." Viv looked as though she were about to cry, but she managed to snuff it out before it escaped. Driving her half-smoked cigarette into a vase filled with sand along with a dozen other butts, she brushed her hands together as if to dismiss that entire part of her life. "There's my next appointment. You both need to go."

I wanted to follow up with her with a few other questions, but Annie shook her head, so we left without another word.

"Do you believe her?" I asked Annie once we were out of the parking lot.

"Yes, without a doubt."

"Why?" I was curious about why my sister had been so willing to take Viv's word without even verifying whether it were true or not.

"She's right. I wouldn't have admitted I was with Mick Roberts unless someone had been holding a gun to my head. I have a feeling that if we ask him, or have Kathleen check around the bar, we'll get confirmation. She just cleared two of our suspects, Pat. At this rate, we'll be out of them by nightfall."

"Assuming everyone has told us the truth, which is one big assumption, that leaves us with Jenna and Robin. Frankly, I can't see either one of them doing it."

"All we can do is play out the hand we've been dealt," Annie said as she drove away.

"Where are we going?"

"We're headed for Robin's house," my sister told me. "We need to figure out a way to get that key without her knowing it. Have you been able to come up with anything?"

"Not so far, but I'm still working on it," I told her.

"Well, work quickly, because we're nearly there."

CHAPTER 18: ANNIE

I HOPED PAT COULD COME UP with something on the spur of the moment. Otherwise, we were going to have to come right out and ask Robin for her key to Timothy's office. Since she was one of our final two suspects, I wasn't all that keen on alarming her. "Are you ready?" I asked my brother as we approached Robin's door.

"I've got this. Just follow my lead," my brother said.

"Do you have a plan at all?"

Pat just gave me two thumbs up and smiled.

That's when I knew we were in trouble.

—◦×◦—

Robin answered right away with a stern look on her face. "Hi. What are you two doing here?" It was a legitimate question, but unfortunately, I didn't have an answer for her.

"We were worried about you," Pat said smoothly. "With all that's been going on, you must be coming unraveled. Is there anything we can do for you?"

Robin's expression softened immediately. "How sweet of you both. Please, come in."

As we did, Pat glanced back at me and winked so Robin couldn't see what he was doing. The rascal had managed to not only get us inside but to soften Robin's attitude toward us as well. Sometimes he amazed me.

"Could I trouble you for a glass of water?" Pat asked as he spied Robin's purse sitting beside the sofa.

"Of course," she said. "Would you like some too, Annie?"

"If it's not too much trouble," I said, making it a point to sit as far away from her bag as I could without looking too suspicious.

"Let me help you," Pat said as he followed her into the kitchen. He was trying to buy me some time, and doing quite a good job of it at that.

As soon as they were in the other room, I started for her purse, only to see Robin's head suddenly pop up from around the corner. "How about tea, instead? I can make us all a fresh pot."

I pretended to stretch before settling back down. "That would be lovely."

"Excellent. I won't be a minute."

Pat showed up for a moment. "Come on, Robin. I'll keep you company."

"It's really not necessary," she protested.

"I insist," he replied with a grin.

It was charming, and Robin felt the full intensity of my brother's attention. He wasn't the most handsome man in the world, or even the smoothest, but he had one thing going for him that few other men had, in my experience. When he gave a woman his attention, she had every last bit of it. Without fail, women found it intoxicating. I was just glad my brother had a kind heart. If he hadn't, he'd have left a trail of broken hearts everywhere he went.

"Come on, then," she said, showing a dimpled little smile.

I had to move quickly. Hurrying across the room, I started digging through her purse looking for her keys. I found her car keys and hoped the office key was with them. There was one door key on the ring, but something wasn't right about it.

I was about to take it anyway when I realized that it had to be the key to Robin's own front door.

So, where was the office key?

Digging around a little more, I tried to navigate the flotsam and jetsam of the woman's life, dodging tissue packets, makeup, loose wrapped candy, and a dozen other things, but still no office key.

"That is so sweet of you," Pat said loudly, much closer than I realized.

They were coming back in, and I still hadn't found the key yet.

By chance alone my fingertips brushed something, and I found a single key with a tag on it. It simply said, "Office," so I knew that I'd finally found it.

The only problem was that I was about to be caught stealing it.

* * *

"That's a lovely dish. It's Depression glass, isn't it?" Pat asked.

The footsteps stopped for a moment, and Robin said, "Yes. I started collecting it as a child. I just love the way the light shines through it, don't you?"

"It's remarkable," he said.

It wasn't much, but it gave me just enough time to close Robin's purse and bolt for my former seat before they came back in.

"Sorry to keep you waiting," Robin said, blushing slightly as she looked at my brother.

"No worries," I said. "I was just catching up on my texts."

"So, how goes the investigation?" she asked as she sat beside her purse.

"These things always take a lot longer than people think," Pat said.

"So, you're no closer than you were before figuring out who did it?" she asked us.

I shrugged. "If anything, we're making even less progress than that. Poor Timothy. I had no idea how many people wished him ill."

"I know. It's staggering to think that such a fine man could attract such questionable clients and acquaintances." Robin quickly added, "Present company excluded, of course."

"Of course," I said as nicely as I could manage despite the dig. "Have you decided what you're going to do with your newfound wealth? Are you still planning on leaving town?"

"Now more than ever," Robin said. "Timothy, through his generosity, has made it possible for me to see the world, and I'm not going to take that gift lightly."

"Of course, the estate can't be settled until his killer his found," Pat said casually.

Robin frowned at him for a moment. "Why on earth not?"

"Until they're certain how he died, and who killed him, they'll hold on to his assets," Pat explained. "After all, they can't have Timothy's estate going to anyone who might have had something to do with his demise."

"Patrick Marsh, are you accusing me of murder?" Robin's face had suddenly gone white.

"No. Of course not. You're not the only one who is set to inherit something. Annie has to be cleared as well before she gets that land. I was speaking in generalities."

"I understand that," Robin said, nodding. "Frankly, I don't care who gets it, as long as it's not Mick. He did it; I know it with all of my heart, even if I can't prove it."

"Normally I would tend to agree with you, but it turns out that he has an alibi," Pat told her.

Robin looked stunned to hear the news. "You don't say. Is it foolproof?"

"I don't know about that, but someone admitted to us that she was with him the night Timothy died, and she seemed pretty adamant about it. Is that something you'd lie about?"

The look of distaste on her face was clear. "Not in a thousand years. Well, you never know, do you? I was certain it was Mick, and I was hoping he'd get what was coming to him."

"Well, at least he won't get any money," I said.

"You mean from Timothy's estate? No, I suppose not, but he's still going to inherit from their father's will," Robin said.

"As a matter of fact, he's not. There's a clause that disallows his inheritance, so their father's assets will be rolled over into Timothy's estate. It appears that you're going to have even more money than you thought."

"Funny, but I never expected any of this," Robin said. "I had no idea my boss would take such good care of me. Still, I'd rather have him here right now than all the money in the world."

"I don't doubt that for one second," Pat said as my cell phone rang.

"Excuse me," I said as I checked to see who was calling me.

It was my brother.

When I glanced over at him, he winked at me. "Yes. Yes. Of course," I said to dead air, since he'd already hung up. How had he managed to do that without either one of us noticing? "I'm sorry, but we need to go."

"Is it about the case?"

"No, it's our family. We'll have to take a rain check on the tea, if you don't mind."

"The invitation is open as long as I'm still in town," Robin said.

———

Outside, I asked my brother, "How did you do that?"

"I set it up to call you when Robin was showing me her Depression glass. I judged it to be the right moment to get us out of there, so I took a chance. That was quick of you to pick up on it."

"Your wink helped," I admitted. "Let's get to that office and back before she notices that I grabbed the key."

"Good. I wasn't sure you got it," Pat said.

I held it up in the air for him to see as we started to get into my car. "It's right here."

———

"What exactly are we looking for?" I asked softly once we let ourselves into the office and locked the door behind us. We skipped Robin's spot out front, and we'd gone straight back to Timothy's inner sanctum.

"Why are you whispering?" Pat asked me with a grin.

"I don't know," I said in my normal voice. "I know this search is for something he had of Jenna's, but I'm not entirely certain what it could be."

"There's only one way to find out," Pat said. "Should we check that filing cabinet again?"

"You start there, and I'll go back out front. We'll have a better chance of finding what we're looking for if we split up."

"Okay. Yell if you find anything."

"How about if I just come get you?" I asked him with a grin. "After all, we don't want to call any attention to the fact that we're here, uninvited."

Pat shrugged. "I'll take my chances."

He disappeared into Timothy's space while I looked around up front. There wasn't anything obvious, and I almost joined my brother when I decided to have a peek in the closet where Robin had hung her coat up when we'd been there with her before. At first all I saw was stacks and stacks of boxes. Surely nothing of importance could be hidden in there, left so unprotected and out in the open like that. I was about to step out and shut the door when I could swear I saw a sliver of light coming from behind one of the stacks. What could that possibly be? I pulled out several boxes, digging deeper and deeper, until I found the source of the light.

It was coming from the other room, Timothy's private—or not so private—office.

I knelt down and looked through the small opening in the paneling and was surprised to find myself watching my brother dig through a filing cabinet!

It was a peephole into Timothy's space, and from it, someone could watch everything the man had been up to! So, that was why Robin had been so overprotective about the closet. I started to call out to Pat when my foot hit one of the nearby boxes I hadn't moved out of the way yet. The lid flipped off, and as I was putting it back in place, I noticed what was inside.

What I found there nearly made me scream.

My brother had to see this.

CHAPTER 19: PAT

ANNIE CAME INTO TIMOTHY'S OFFICE with a grim look on her face as she carried a storage box in her arms. "What's going on, sis?" I asked her.

Instead of answering, she placed the box on Timothy's desk and flipped the lid over.

I looked inside and was startled to find image after image of Timothy, both from the office and at his cabin. It was clear by the composition of the shots that he'd had no idea he'd been under surveillance.

"How did she manage to take these?" I asked Annie incredulously.

"There's a peephole in the closet, and I can only assume she had some kind of camera rigged up at the cabin, too."

"I can't believe this," I said.

"See for yourself. It's easy to spot after I moved the boxes out of the way."

"I'm not calling you a liar, but this I need to see with my own two eyes." I walked up front, made my way through the maze of boxes stacked randomly outside the closet door, and walked inside. The hole was easy enough to spot. I knelt down and peered inside.

Annie waved. "Peekaboo," she said.

"Unbelievable," I replied. "I'll be right there."

That's when I felt the cold steel from a gun barrel poke me in the neck.

"Take it nice and easy, Pat," the familiar voice said. "Let's go out and join your sister."

CHAPTER 20: ANNIE

I STARTED TO SAY SOMETHING AS Pat came into the office, but the words died in my throat when I saw Robin Jenkins standing behind him, a gun pointed at my brother's head.

"You two think you're so cute," she said. "Did you honestly think I wouldn't notice that the key was gone as soon as you left? It was the first thing I checked. Lucky for me, I had Timothy's key, too. I was going to use it to incriminate someone else, but I wasn't sure who to pick once Mick disqualified himself. I'm glad I waited now."

"We can explain," Pat started to say, and then Robin jammed the barrel into his neck a little harder.

"Save it," she answered. "Get over there with your sister."

Pat did as he was told, and as he approached me, he said softly, "I'm so sorry."

"You couldn't help it any more than I could," I said, doing my best to console him. We might be about to die, but I wasn't going to let it happen with any hard feelings between us.

"You two need to shut up right now," Robin said angrily, "while I figure out what to do with you. You've messed up my plans, so I need to come up with a new scenario."

"You could always just let us go," I suggested.

"That's not likely to happen, Annie. What tipped you off, anyway? I thought I was careful covering my tracks."

I wasn't about to tell her that we'd come in search of Jenna's secret, not hers. Why give her the satisfaction? "Finding all of that key evidence in one file drawer was awfully convenient," I said, realizing that it was true. The moment I knew that Robin had killed Timothy, things began to fall into place. "The typed list of suspects and motives was almost too good to believe. Then waiting to point out the will that left it all to you was another nice touch, but I think the thing I liked the most was that note from Timothy to you. You faked that as well, didn't you?"

"Why would you say that?" she asked me with a frown. "He admired me."

"Good try, but Timothy's portion was typed, while yours was written in your own handwriting," I explained.

"Plus, Timothy's notes were all typed as well," Pat added. "You went to that well one too many times. Did you forge his signature on the will? Why not copy the rest of his handwriting?"

"I'd practiced his signature enough, but there was no way I could fake an entire document."

"It was a nice touch leaving me his property," I said.

"The truth of the matter is that part was real enough. The land and the secondary bequest were both legitimate."

"Why don't I believe you?" I asked.

"If I were stupid enough to let you go, you could always see for yourself. The real will is in my desk in the Shred folder."

"Just out of curiosity, who was the real beneficiary?"

"Jenna," she said, as though it were a curse. "He never changed his will, but after I take care of the two of you, no one will ever know. At first, I tried to pin it on Mick, and if that didn't work, Viv and Gordon were likely candidates as well. Jenna was my last resort, besides you two, that is."

"Why the fire?" Pat asked her.

"I thought it would get rid of my fingerprints. It worked, too. I'm curious about something myself. I know that fire at the Iron was burning this morning when I left. What happened?"

"I spotted it and put it out," Pat admitted.

She wasn't happy about that at all. "Okay, not everything worked out the way I planned it to."

"Robin, *all* of your carefully laid plans were foiled. Since we're not going to get out of this alive, tell me one last thing," I asked her.

"What's that? Make it quick. I won't be put off from getting rid of both of you."

"Why did you kill Timothy in the first place?" I asked her, sincerely wanting to know the truth before my brother and I died.

"He rejected me one too many times," she said bitterly. "I knew he and Jenna were breaking up, and I didn't want to waste any time. I had a suspicion that he'd go crawling back to you if I didn't do something, so I drove out to his cabin and declared my love for him."

"How did he react to that?" Pat asked.

"He laughed at me! I couldn't believe it! I told him I was leaving, and he went to get my coat from the closet. It didn't take much to close the door, lock it, and jam a chair under the knob for good measure. He thought I was kidding! You should have heard him pounding on that door trying to get out. I decided that I wasn't going to take his humiliating treatment for another moment, so I splashed some gasoline around and lit it! You need to be careful, Annie. It's amazing how quickly wooden cabins catch on fire."

I could almost see the flames dancing in her eyes as she described the scene. Poor Timothy. Nobody deserved to die trapped like a cornered rat as the flames and smoke got closer and closer. "How are you going to explain us?" I asked her.

"What do you mean?"

"You can't make it look as though it were simply another accident, and you've set entirely too many fires for that to work again."

"Maybe I can manage something a little less elegant," she said with a wicked grin. "How about this? You two broke into the place, the real killer caught you, and then shot you both. I think you're wrong about having another fire. It seems to match the pattern, doesn't it? The killer will burn this place down, too. Fire is such a cleansing thing, isn't it?" There was true madness in her now.

Robin might be able to shoot one of us, but I doubted she'd be able to get both of us before we acted.

We had no choice in the matter. One of us had to make a move.

Hopefully, I could draw her fire long enough for Pat to jump her and disarm her. No matter what happened to me, I needed my brother to survive the encounter. Robin couldn't get away with killing so many people without being punished for any of it.

I was about to jump toward her when I saw Pat tense.

He was going to try to do the same thing!

I had to stop him, but I didn't know how.

Fortunately, there was a sudden pounding on the front door behind Robin.

The cold-blooded killer made the mistake of instinctively turning her head toward the sound for a split second.

And that was all we needed.

CHAPTER 21: PAT

I saw Annie tensing up to leap forward, and I knew that I had to do it before she could. My crazy sister was trying to save me! I appreciated the sentiment, but there was no way I was going to live with the guilt of her sacrificing herself for me.

I started to jump first when I heard someone pounding heavily on the front door of the office.

Robin glanced back for a second, and Annie and I made our moves simultaneously, as though we'd rehearsed it a thousand times before.

She tried to take Robin's legs out from under her while I went for the gun.

Annie scored a direct hit, but as Robin stumbled back under the impact of my sister's expert tackle, the gun lowered toward her, and I knew that I wasn't going to make it in time.

CHAPTER 22: ANNIE

I SAW THE GUN COMING TOWARD my head, and I knew that Pat and I had mistimed our attack. At least she wouldn't be able to get us both.

———◆⊙◆———

Then Kathleen burst into the room. In a motion that was almost surreal, I saw her point the revolver in her hand directly at Robin's heart as she shouted, "Drop it. I'll shoot you in a heartbeat if it's between you and my family."

Robin hesitated a moment, and then the gun in her hand fell down onto the carpet beside me.

It was over, and my twin brother and I had somehow both managed to survive it.

———◆⊙◆———

"How did you even know where we were?" I asked our older sister once Robin had been cuffed and led away by one of Kathleen's officers. "Were you following us?"

"Don't flatter yourself," she said with a wry grin. "I had a hunch Robin wasn't as innocent as she wanted us to believe, so I've been tailing her for the past few hours. Imagine my surprise when I saw you two show up at her place earlier."

"You knew she was one of our suspects," Pat said.

"Sure, but I didn't realize how right you were until I saw her follow you soon after you left her house. It didn't take a genius to figure out where you were all going."

"If you were there that long, why didn't you come in sooner?" I asked our older sister. I hadn't meant to be accusatory, but it must have sounded that way to her.

"Annie, I wasn't sure what was going on. By the time I figured it out, it was almost too late. I could hear you all talking from outside, but I knew I couldn't risk just barging in. I cracked the door enough to see her holding a gun on you both through the doorway, but I couldn't chance a shot going past her and hitting one of you. I figured pounding on the doorframe might distract her enough to give me a free shot. I never dreamed you two would try to tackle her yourselves."

"In our defense, we didn't know you were just outside," I told her. "Thanks for coming to our rescue."

"I have a hunch you would have been fine without me."

I remembered how close that gun had come to my head and shuddered. "Trust me, sis, we needed you."

"Well, it all worked out in the end. Like I said, I heard bits and pieces of it from outside. She was really spying on him at work and at home?"

"Crazy, isn't it?" Pat asked as he showed her the box he'd found. "We came here looking for something of Jenna's and ended up catching a killer. Speaking of which," Pat said as he walked past our sister, went to Robin's desk, and pulled out the Shred file. Inside, he found something quickly and held it out to Kathleen. "There's the real will. Annie still gets the property, but Jenna inherits everything else. Timothy's will, like the note and the list we found, were all forged."

"Well, well. I wonder if Jenna has any idea of what's about to happen?"

"Any idea about what?" the woman herself asked as she joined us. "What's going on?"

"Why are you here?" Pat asked her.

"I decided to come by and find the letters I'd written to Timothy myself."

"So, you were telling us the truth," Pat said.

Her lips formed two thin lines before she replied, "Imagine that."

"No worries," Kathleen said. "They're locked up safely in my desk drawer. I figured you'd want to destroy them yourself. Don't worry, I didn't read them, at least not after I realized what they were."

"That's at least something," Jenna said. "Thank you for sparing me the embarrassment."

"There's more. It turns out that you're going to be rich," Kathleen said.

"What are you talking about?" Jenna asked her.

It was clear she had no idea what my big sister meant. It took a few moments for it to sink in, even after she'd read the fine print herself, but once it had, she let the will fall from her hands to the floor. "It doesn't really matter now, does it?"

"What do you mean? Don't you want the money?" Kathleen asked her.

"Sure. Why not? You know something? It might be just what I need for a fresh start somewhere else."

"You're leaving town?" Pat asked her incredulously.

"Is there any reason I shouldn't? There's nothing left for me here. Is there?"

The question hung in the air much longer than it must have felt, until Pat answered softly, "No. I guess not."

Jenna didn't even look all that surprised by his response. "Then it's settled."

The vet turned and walked out without once asking what we'd all been doing there.

It was the close of not just a chapter but an entire book.

Jenna was moving on, and out of all of our lives, including my brother's, once and for all.

CHAPTER 23: PAT

A FEW DAYS LATER, THINGS WERE finally getting back to normal at the Iron, something I was eternally grateful for.

Skip approached me and asked, "Pat, do you have a second?"

"Sure, what's up?"

"I've finally got the display just the way I want," he said. He'd been working on it off and on since I'd given him my approval, and I was eager to see his final version.

It actually turned out to be more than I'd expected. Not satisfied with his display of snowmen and trees alone, Skip had turned one shelf into a virtual winter wonderland. He'd used fake snow, created a rolling hill as a backdrop, and he'd even formed a tableau featuring snowmen and decorated trees spread throughout an idealistic winter scene. "What do you think?"

"It's almost too pretty to break up and sell," I told him honestly.

"That's the beauty of it. We don't have to."

"What do you mean?"

"I've been making the individual components, but I've also done a full display piece that matches this exactly. Think how pretty it will be on people's mantles, tabletops, even windowsills. Check this out," he added with a grin as he reached down and flipped on a switch. The entire scene was now bathed in bluish-white LCD light, something that reminded me of snowy winter evenings from my childhood.

"It's the best thing you've ever done," I said as I patted him on the back.

"Really? Do you mean that?"

"I do," I said. "In fact, I want to cancel my earlier order." Before he could misunderstand my intent, I added quickly, "I want three of the new sets; one for Annie, one for Kathleen, and one to keep for myself."

"You've got it, boss," he said happily. "I can't wait for the first snowfall."

"I don't know. I'm happy with today, and the hope there will be a tomorrow on its heels. Everything else is just icing on the cake, as far as I'm concerned."

As Skip went up front to wait on a customer, I glanced back at Annie, happily working the grill. Knowing how close we'd come to losing everything, it gave me a renewed sense of appreciation for every day that we had and a desire to get every ounce of life out of every moment.

Maybe I'd even have that long-overdue chat with Molly about seeing if we could try again.

But not today.

———— ✦ ————

Today was fine, just the way it was.

RECIPES

Artisan Bread Baked in a Cast Iron Dutch Oven

I was amazed by how wonderful this bread recipe turned out the very first time I tried it. Since I always play with everything I make in the kitchen, always searching for that perfect combination, I've reworked this half a dozen times until I am quite pleased with the results. It's easy to make (not a no-knead but a little knead), doesn't take many ingredients, and results in a delightful bread that you'll swear was created by a master baker! As an added bonus, the house smells wonderful all day. This method steams the bread as it bakes, resulting in a crispy crust and an interior that is reminiscent of sourdough with its delightful tenderness! Try this one. You won't be disappointed! If you like white bread, just use all regular bread flour (1½ cups) and omit the wheat entirely!

Note: The recipe can be doubled without a problem, but now that our nest is empty, we're happy with a loaf made for just two people, which is what is presented here.

Ingredients
- 1 cup bread flour
- 1/2 cup whole wheat flour
- 1/2 teaspoon salt
- 1⁄4 teaspoon yeast (I use regular yeast, not rapid rise, for this recipe)
- 3/4 cup water (heated to 110 degrees F)

Directions

In a large mixing bowl, add the bread flour, wheat flour, salt, and yeast and stir together well. Next, heat the water until it is approximately 110 degrees F. In my microwave, it's 32 seconds on high, but your mileage may vary. Add the hot water to the mix, stirring it well until it is mostly incorporated. Turn the dough onto a floured surface and knead about fifteen times. The dough will be warm and sticky, but that's as it should be at this point. Next, place the dough in a bowl sprayed with nonstick vegetable spray, cover with plastic wrap, and set aside for three hours. When that time is up, place your cast iron Dutch oven in a cold oven and raise the temperature to 450 degrees F. Give it half an hour to allow the cast iron to reach the desired temperature as well, which takes a little longer than the oven itself. As the cast iron is preheating, place the dough on the floured surface and knead five or six times for good measure. Cover with the bowl it rose in and wait. Carefully remove the hot Dutch oven after the half hour is up, remove the lid, spray the bottom with nonstick vegetable spray, and turn to your dough. Make three cuts across the top to allow expansion, then flour your hands and drop the dough directly into the hot Dutch oven. Replace the cover and put the entire thing back into the oven. Bake for 16 to 18 minutes, then remove the lid only! Allow the bread to brown in the open Dutch oven for 5 to 8 minutes until golden brown and crispy. Remove the bread from the oven and cool on a rack for 5 to 10 minutes before cutting. Enjoy!

Serves two people, with a little left over if neither one of you is too greedy!

Pumpkin Waffles

We love pumpkin waffles at our house, no matter what time of year it might be. They are rich and hearty, tasty, and truly delightful. Enhancing a box waffle mix, we like to add pumpkin, extra eggs, vanilla, and instant oats to create a breakfast that really sticks with you. I often make a double batch, and if there are any left, they freeze great. I double wrap them to protect them from freezer burn, and when I'm ready for a waffle or two, I simply pop them in the toaster, still frozen, and soon I have a wonderful breakfast delight that I consider homemade despite starting with a boxed mix! We started out making pumpkin pancakes and decided one day to try it with our waffle mix, with outstanding success!

Ingredients

- 3 cups waffle mix
- 3 eggs, beaten
- 1 cup water
- 1 cup canned pumpkin
- 2/3 cup quick oats (raw)
- 1/4 cup canola oil
- 1 tablespoon vanilla extract
- 1 teaspoon cinnamon
- 1 teaspoon nutmeg

Directions

Turn on your waffle iron, or set an old-fashioned one on your burner to preheat, spraying with nonstick vegetable spray first. In a large bowl, combine the waffle mix, eggs, water, pumpkin, oats, canola oil, vanilla, cinnamon, and nutmeg, mixing just until everything is incorporated. Set the mix aside for 2 to 3 minutes, and then add ½ to ¾ cup of the mixture at a time to the heated iron. Cook for 3½ to 4 minutes, or until they reach a rich pumpkin gold, and serve. These are tasty plain but really soar when coupled with butter and syrup.

Makes four to six waffles, depending on the amount of batter you drop each time.

If you enjoy Jessica Beck Mysteries and you would like to be notified when the next book is being released, please send your email address to **newreleases@jessicabeckmysteries.net**. Your email address will not be shared, sold, bartered, traded, broadcast, or disclosed in any way. There will be no spam from us, just a friendly reminder when the latest book is being released.

Also, be sure to visit our website at jessicabeckmysteries.net for valuable information about Jessica's books.

OTHER BOOKS BY JESSICA BECK

The Donut Mysteries
Glazed Murder
Fatally Frosted
Sinister Sprinkles
Evil Éclairs
Tragic Toppings
Killer Crullers
Drop Dead Chocolate
Powdered Peril
Illegally Iced
Deadly Donuts
Assault and Batter
Sweet Suspects
Deep Fried Homicide
Custard Crime
Lemon Larceny
Bad Bites
Old Fashioned Crooks
Dangerous Dough
Troubled Treats
Sugar Coated Sins
Criminal Crumbs
Vanilla Vices
Raspberry Revenge
Fugitive Filling
Devil's Food Defense
Pumpkin Pleas

The Classic Diner Mysteries
A Chili Death

A Deadly Beef
A Killer Cake
A Baked Ham
A Bad Egg
A Real Pickle
A Burned Biscuit

The Ghost Cat Cozy Mysteries
Ghost Cat: Midnight Paws
Ghost Cat 2: Bid for Midnight

The Cast Iron Cooking Mysteries
Cast Iron Will
Cast Iron Conviction
Cast Iron Alibi
Cast Iron Motive
Cast Iron Suspicion

Made in the USA
Coppell, TX
19 October 2019